Covenant of Silence Saga
Book I

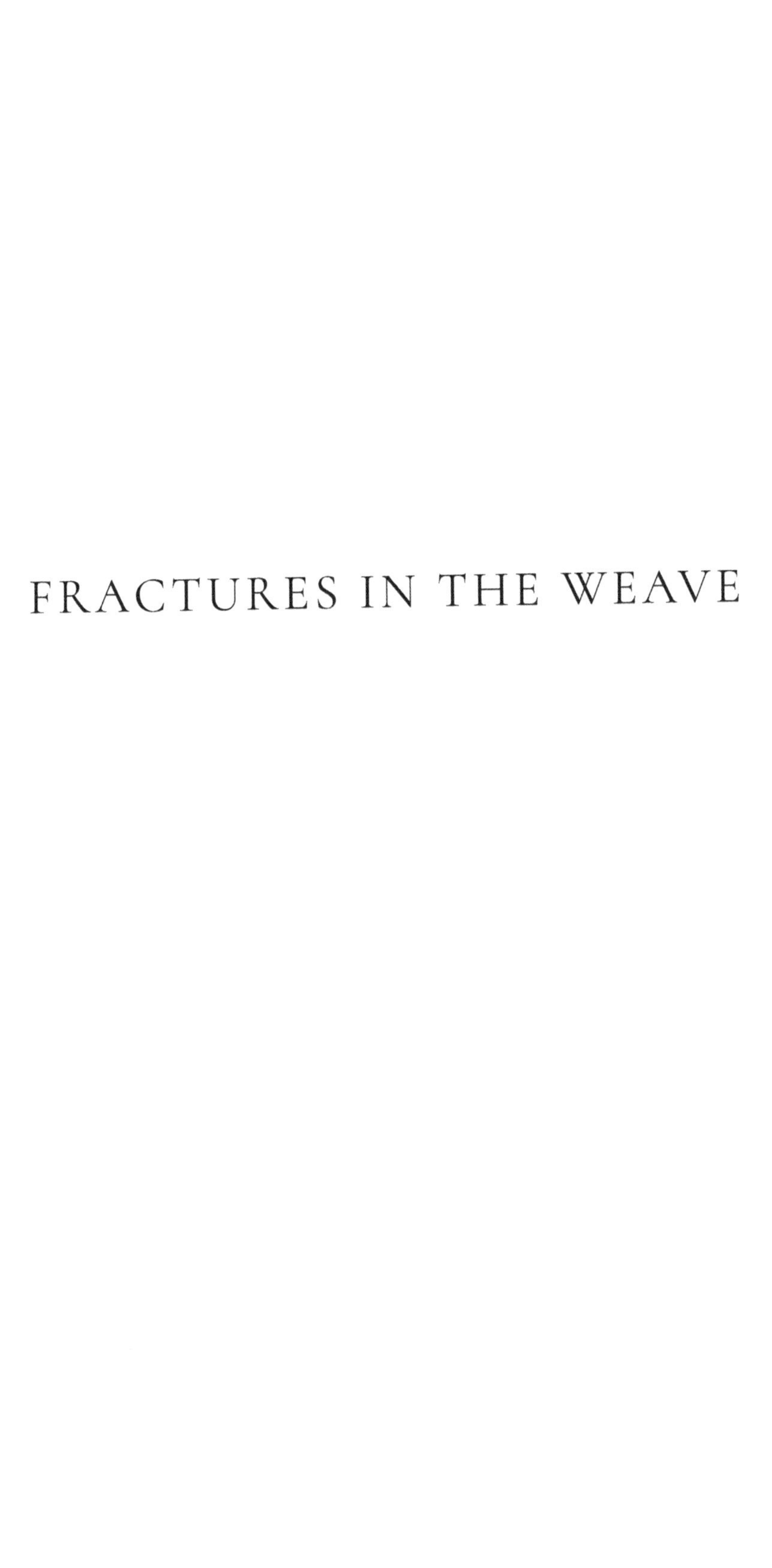

FRACTURES IN THE WEAVE

FRACTURES IN THE WEAVE

JOHN D JENNETT

Contents

For my wife Christy, her love and support made everything possible.

1

The Fracture

The night was pitch-black. The stars struggled to pierce the heavy mantle of clouds draped over Minneapolis. Four men rode in a plain blue van that moved silently through the empty streets in the predawn hours.

This would be a night all Americans would remember, the night that marked the beginning of their end.

Inside the van, the men spoke in Pashtu, their faces hard with grim determination. Abdul lifted the tarp and checked the device one last time. The others sat in silence, listening to the hum of the engine and the steady rhythm of their own hearts.

The van pulled into the parking garage off 3rd Street by the Convention Center downtown. Finding a shadowed corner on the first level, Lateef and Jawwad stepped out, pretending to inspect the engine, their breath ghosting in the cold air. Inside, Abdul and Mohammad worked over the device, ensuring every connection was perfect.

There was little room in the back; the machine consumed nearly all the space. Abdul's eyes lingered on the yellow-and-black nuclear symbol stenciled on the steel casing.

"Allāhu akbar," he whispered, pressing the final sequence of numbers.

The explosion vaporized the parking garage in a heartbeat. The nuclear fireball bloomed outward, devouring everything it touched. Concrete, steel, and glass turned to ash in the blink of an eye. The shockwave ripped through the city, its roar louder than thunder, faster than thought,

Then time stopped.

Silence.

The blinding light hung suspended in the air, motionless, frozen like a painting. The fireball began to collapse inward, pulling smoke, debris, and shattered buildings back into itself. Cars reassembled. Windows mended. People were once again asleep in their beds, unaware of the destruction that had almost been.

The swirling light folded into a single brilliant point, and for an instant, a towering female figure appeared at its heart, long hair and robes streaming as if caught in an invisible storm.

Then came a boom like the breath of creation.

The van, the four men, and the figure vanished. Only the echo of car alarms filled the quiet night.

Someone, or something, had decided enough was enough.
***

In a vast chamber encircled by an ancient stone wall, a bottomless well glowed with the slow, steady rotation of a miniature Earth. The carvings along the rim shimmered with light from no visible source. Five figures stood around the well, their faces grave as they watched the world turn.

"You should not have done that, Kemen," said Vilya, his voice heavy with reproach. "We swore an oath of non-interference."

Kemen, tall and radiant, turned toward him. Her hair shimmered like burnished bronze in the dim light. "I can no longer stand by and watch them destroy each other for no reason," she said fiercely. "They must learn to live and let live."

Vilya's expression darkened. "Century after century, they kill each other, and still you hope they will change?"

Kemen's brown eyes blazed. "Hope is all that keeps their world turning."

The sphere of Earth spun silently between them, fragile and luminous in the dark.

It began as a tremor, small, silent, invisible.
Not in the earth, but beneath it.

In the hidden lattice that bound creation, a single strand quivered. It was so slight that even the immortals did not feel it at first. The pulse spread slowly, rippling outward through the unseen veins that once carried magic like blood through the body of the world.

Then came the shiver in the dark.

It rippled through the oceans, and whales turned their heads toward unseen currents. It whispered through forests, and the oldest trees straightened as if hearing a forgotten song.

In the deserts, wind lifted sheets of dust that shimmered faintly blue before settling again.
In the cities, streetlights flickered in unison, though no power lines had failed.

Something vast was waking.

Far above, in the chamber of the Well, Kemen stood at the rim and felt it at last, the first thread breaking loose. The miniature Earth below her spun faster, its surface spider-webbed with faint lines of light. They pulsed once, twice, then began to glow with dangerous beauty.

"Vilya," she whispered. "Do you feel it?"

The others appeared around her, faces carved with unease. The Well's glow climbed the walls, bathing the ancient runes in spectral fire.

"The seal is fracturing," Beagron said, voice low as thunder. "Your interference stirred it."

Kemen didn't answer. Her gaze was fixed on the globe. From Minneapolis outward, a thin filament of light spread, cutting across continents like lightning through glass. Each pulse widened the cracks, bleeding radiance into the void.

"It was bound by silence," Vilya murmured. "But silence cannot hold forever."

Below them, the Weave exhaled.

The faint hum that had always lingered at the edge of hearing swelled into a chord that filled every corner of the chamber. The Earth's rotation blurred into a whirl of light and shadow, threads of magic uncoiling, spilling into the human world.

In that instant, every barrier they had raised twenty millennia ago shuddered. The old language, the one spoken by rivers, stone, and stars, whispered its first syllables again.

The Weave did not roar or burn.

It *breathed.*

Across the planet, animals froze and turned their heads toward the horizon.

The auroras bent toward the equator.

The air thickened, alive with static.

In a Tennessee valley, a creek began to glow faintly blue under the moon.

In New Mexico, a dust storm changed direction without wind.

In Chicago, a woman's heart pounded in rhythm with another's grief.

In Miami, a young woman dreamed of fire.

In San Francisco, data lines hummed with voices that were not human.

The Weave had broken, and the breath of magic slipped through the cracks.

In the chamber above the world, Kemen closed her eyes. Her bronze hair lifted as the air around her trembled with unseen currents.

"It's begun," Cylian said quietly, her expression rippling with the same pain that trembled through the wounded Weave.

"Yes," Kemen whispered. "And this time, the world will remember."

Below her, the glowing sphere shone with the light of ten thousand intersecting threads, each one newly alive, each one carrying a name that had not yet been spoken.

The silence was over. The Weave was singing again.

2

Woodlawn

Morning came before light. Ethan Moore was already awake when the alarm stayed silent. He didn't need it anymore; his body was trained, five a.m., every day, without fail.

He lay still for a moment, listening. The house creaked softly around him, boards settling in the chill. Outside, the world hadn't decided to wake yet. That narrow hush before dawn, that was his hour. No voices. No memories that could reach him.

He swung his legs over the side of the bed, feet touching the cold floor. His knees protested the way they always did. He rubbed them once, out of habit more than comfort.

He dressed by rote: jeans, thermal shirt, worn boots. The motions were slow, deliberate, small pieces of control that kept the rest at bay.

He moved through the house on autopilot, checking windows, doors, and corners. Each latch, each curtain edge, a mental checkpoint. Nothing was out of place. Nothing waiting in the dark.

Not paranoia. Muscle memory.

He brewed coffee next, the old pot grumbled like it resented being woken too. The smell hit him first: bitter, earthy, real. He watched the first dark stream fill the mug, rising like smoke, and took a deep breath.

He drank it black. Always had. Sweet things felt dishonest.

Outside, dawn crawled slow over the field. Mist hugged the grass, curling in faint ribbons that caught the weak light. The air was damp, cold enough to sting his throat.

The creek down past the barn whispered through the trees, a soft and steady sound that belonged here more than he ever had. That murmur was the one thing he liked about the place, calm, constant, not asking anything of him.

He tossed feed to the chickens, their fussing sharp against the quiet. They crowded around his boots, pecking, flapping, messy, alive. For a second, he thought of the barracks. The noise, the closeness, the way laughter used to fill the empty spaces between missions. He caught himself almost smiling. Then the memory shifted, sand, sun, and shouting. He blinked it away.

He split wood next. The rhythm helped, grip, swing, breathe, repeat. The echo rolled down the hollow with every strike, grounding him. Sweat cooled on his neck.

Then one swing came down too hard. The sound cracked sharper than it should have, echoing like a gunshot.

For an instant, the Tennessee woods vanished.

He was back under the Afghan sun, heat and dust burning his lungs. The ground shuddered, the air metallic with blood and powder. Someone screamed "Medic!" and he was already moving, hands pressed against a wound that wouldn't stop leaking through his fingers.

The smell of iron. The ringing in his ears. That ringing again.

Ethan froze mid-motion, axe gripped tight. The world narrowed to that high, piercing whine, no creek, no birds, just that old noise that made his heart stumble.

He shut his eyes and forced himself to breathe.

Four things you can see. Three you can touch. Two you can hear. One you can smell.

The old grounding drill.

He opened his eyes. The creek murmured again. The wind moved in the grass.

He was home.

The axe dropped from his hands, landing heavy in the dirt. His shirt clung to his back, soaked through.

He stood there a long while, head bowed, breathing hard until his heartbeat stopped trying to break free of his chest.

By the time the sun burned the fog off, the day looked calm again. Mist lifted from the fields in thin silver trails. It would've been peaceful, if not for the ghosts it left behind.

He washed up at the kitchen sink, watching dirt swirl down the drain. The face in the mirror above the counter didn't surprise him anymore, lined, tired, beard going more gray than black. He wasn't old, but he looked like he'd lived through more years than he'd earned.

This place was supposed to fix that. To quiet it. But after three years alone on five acres, all it had done was make the silence louder.

Around noon, he drove into town for supplies. Woodlawn wasn't much, one diner, one gas station, a post office the size of a storage shed and a veterinary clinic.

The truck rattled along the cracked road, radio off. He preferred the quiet.

At the gas station, the clerk greeted him with a nod. Ethan returned it, nothing more. People in town had learned not to push conversation on him. He was polite, but distant. Someone you waved to, not talked at.

"Looks like rain," the clerk said, glancing at the clouds bruising the sky.

Ethan nodded. "Smells like it."

The air had that heavy taste, a metallic weight before a storm. Something was coming.

Driving back, he passed the church on the corner, white siding, paint flaking from years of Tennessee weather. The sign out front read: *GOD SPEAKS IN STILLNESS.*

He almost laughed. If God was speaking, He'd been whispering to someone else.

Back home, Ethan stacked the firewood he'd split earlier. His muscles hummed from the work, a good ache, clean and earned.

He sat on the porch with another mug of coffee, watching the light shift. The cicadas rose and fell in their endless song, the creek's low voice threading through. For a while, it felt almost peaceful.

Then the wind shifted.

It swept through the hollow with a sudden force that set the trees groaning. The chickens went silent. The air carried that same metallic tang again, sharper now, electric, like the taste before lightning strikes.

And beneath it, faint but clear, a whisper.

"Ethan."

He stiffened. The sound came from the tree line, or maybe from everywhere at once. He scanned the yard. Nothing moved except the tall grass, bending in slow waves.

He waited, listening. Nothing. Just wind.

He told himself it was nothing, the mind playing tricks, the same as before.

But when he tried to sit again, the chair creaked under him like it wasn't sure either.

Rain came in steady sheets by nightfall. The kind that drowned out thought if you let it, hammering against the roof like a thousand small fists. Ethan sat in the darkened living room, the TV on mute, watching the local weather crawl across the bottom of the screen. Clarksville under flood warning. High winds along the Cumberland.

Didn't matter much to him. The house was solid. The barn roof might leak again, but that was tomorrow's problem.

He rubbed the scar that ran from his left wrist to the base of his thumb, a habit more than a thought and listened to the wind find the cracks in the siding. Somewhere out back, the old wind chime clattered against the porch post. It had hung there since he bought the place, tarnished brass bells on frayed rope. He'd meant to take it down a dozen times, but somehow it always stayed.

Thunder rolled deep over the hills. The kind that carried a low vibration through the floorboards. It stirred something familiar in him, something from another world, convoys under a dark sky, the thump of rotors coming in low, dust and diesel, the smell of cordite.

He shut his eyes.

The memory came quick, uninvited.

A stretch of highway outside Kandahar. Convoy lights dimmed, red filters on, the world narrowed to silhouettes and the steady drone of engines. Then...

White light. Heat.

The crack that splits the world.

Screams, metal twisting.

He was back in his living room again, breathing too shallow, the rain still tapping the windows. His hand had tightened into a fist without meaning to.

"Jesus," he whispered.

He stood, crossed the room, and checked the locks again. Once, twice. Every window. He told himself it was for the storm, but it wasn't.

The whisper came then. Soft, almost buried in the wind.

At first he thought it was just the house shifting. Wood swelling from the damp, gutters rattling loose. But then it came again; low, drawn out, somewhere between breath and speech.

Ethan froze.

It sounded like *his name*.

He stood there in the half-dark, heart climbing into his throat, waiting for it to come again. When it didn't, he exhaled through his teeth and told himself he was overtired. That's all. Working too long on the land, too quiet for too many days. You start hearing things when there's no one to talk to but the wind.

Still, he went to the window.

The field beyond the creek was a haze of rain, dark grass bending under the gusts. The barn's shape loomed against the lightning, black and familiar. Nothing out of place. But the longer he stood there, the more the feeling grew, like the air itself was waiting for something.

He turned off the muted TV, grabbed his flashlight, and killed the lights. Habit.

It was almost peaceful in the dark. The house became part of the storm, groaning, breathing, alive.

He poured two fingers of bourbon, sat at the kitchen table, and let the sound fill the room. He tried to make sense of the whisper. The mind finds patterns where it wants to, he knew that. But there had been *tone* in it, something almost human. Not words, but intent.

Lightning flared again, lighting the yard white for an instant. The reflection caught in the window, his own face ghosted against the glass, eyes hollow, jaw clenched. He looked like someone half-gone.

He thought of what the VA counselor had said once, years back: *You're chasing silence in a world that doesn't have any.*

Maybe she'd been right.

He sat there until the bourbon was gone and the storm shifted east. The whisper didn't come again, but it stayed in him, the shape of it, the way it had leaned toward his name.

When he finally went to bed, he couldn't sleep. Every time he closed his eyes, the rain became static, the static became a voice, and the voice was asking him something he couldn't make out.

Near dawn, the wind fell still. The silence that followed was worse. It wasn't calm. It was *expectant.*

Ethan lay awake, staring at the ceiling, pulse steady but cold.

Something had changed.

He couldn't say how he knew, only that the world outside his window didn't feel the same.

The world was washed clean by morning.

A pale light stretched through the trees, soft and cold, the kind that follows a long storm. Ethan stood at the kitchen window, mug in hand, watching the fog drift low over the pasture and along the creek that cut through the back of his land. The water ran high and fast, carrying bits of leaves and broken twigs downstream.

The quiet was heavy.

No birds yet, no hum of insects, just the muted rush of the swollen creek. The kind of silence that pressed on the chest and made every breath sound too loud.

He drank his coffee slowly, eyes tracking the gray light moving across the wet fields. Everything looked ordinary enough, but something in him said it wasn't. The unease from last night still clung to him, faint but constant, like the smell of smoke after it's gone out.

He set the mug down, pulled on his jacket, and stepped outside.

The air was sharp with the scent of rain and mud. Gravel shifted under his boots as he crossed the yard toward the treeline. The storm had left its mark, branches scattered, a section of gutter pulled loose, a few shingles lying in the grass. He took it in automatically, mind already cataloguing what needed repair.

But it wasn't the house he was worried about.

Down by the creek, something had changed.

He noticed it as he drew closer, a stretch of bank torn up, the mud churned like something heavy had pressed up through it. The water there moved strangely, not in smooth ripples but in wide, circling eddies that spun against the current.

Ethan crouched at the edge, flashlight in hand even though dawn had already broken. The smell hit him first, clean and sharp, but under it, something metallic, faintly electric. He brushed a hand along the torn mud. It wasn't soft the way rain runoff made it; it was firm, as if molded, pressed into a shape that wanted to hold.

A circular depression. Too even to be natural.

He leaned closer, frowning. No tracks. No tire marks from passing farm trucks. The ground nearby was untouched.

He straightened slowly, eyes on the flowing water. The surface glimmered dull silver under the morning light, carrying pieces of bark and foam down toward the next bend. For a second, he thought he saw something flash beneath, a faint pulse of blue, but when he blinked, it was gone.

He stayed there, still as a post, until the sound of the current seemed to fill his whole head.

"Not today," he muttered finally, voice low.

He turned back toward the barn. The door hung slightly open, swaying on its hinge. He knew he'd latched it before the storm.

Inside, the air smelled of wet hay and oil. Sunlight pierced through the boards in narrow, dusty lines. His tools were all in place, tractor under its tarp. Nothing touched, except for one thing.

The wind chime.

The old brass chime that usually hung from the porch beam now dangled from a nail driven into a barn post. It moved faintly in the still air, the soft clink of metal carrying longer than it should.

Ethan stopped. The rope looked newly tied, damp, and clean. He hadn't moved it.

He stared at it for a long time, the silence pressing tighter, until the sound seemed to echo not through the barn but *inside him*. He reached up, stilled the chime with one hand, and caught that same smell, ozone, faint and cold, like the air before lightning strikes.

He backed away.

The fog outside had thickened, curling low through the grass, shifting with slow purpose toward the creek.

He watched it gather along the bank, listened to the soft churn of the water.

The storm was gone, but whatever it had brought with it, that wasn't.

3

The Dying Dog

Ethan took a drive to clear his head. The truck's tires hummed against the damp asphalt. Fog rolled off the fields in ghostly curls, clinging to the low ridges, curling around fence posts like restless spirits. Ethan's hands gripped the wheel; knuckles pale under the tension he didn't even notice at first. He didn't want to think, didn't want to remember, but his body carried its own memory, muscles tight with anticipation.

Out of the mist, something dark and unmoving sprawled along the side of the road. At first, he thought it was a bag, someone had dumped trash again. But the shape shifted subtly, too deliberate, too organic.

He slammed on the brakes, heart jumping.

A dog. Small, tan with mottled fur, legs splayed at impossible angles, blood soaking the roadside. Its chest barely rose with a shallow, shallow breath. Ethan froze.

He knelt beside it, hands hovering for a moment above the fur matted with grime and blood. He didn't breathe. His mind skipped backward, instant replay: the firefight at Chora, screaming over the comms, bodies missing limbs, the smell of smoke and sweat and earth.

He swallowed hard. Not here. Not now.

But he had no choice. The dog was alive, barely, and waiting.

He flipped the dog onto his lap, careful to keep pressure off its legs. It whimpered. Small, pathetic, and already bending toward death. He pressed his hands against its chest, instinct overriding rational thought. CPR. Just like the training, just like the medics drilled him over and over, except here, it wasn't a man, it was a dog, and the rules seemed to falter under the fog of fear.

Hands shaking, he pressed again. Nothing. Chest flat. No pulse.

Ethan's jaw tightened. He thought of the men he couldn't save, the ones who burned into memory like a brand. This shouldn't have happened. He shouldn't have failed again.

Another press. And then, a spark.

Warmth flared in his palms, a surge like liquid fire running through his veins, climbing his forearms, setting his heart hammering in response. He froze, eyes wide, mouth open. It shouldn't be happening. Adrenaline? Heat stroke? A hallucination brought on by guilt?

The dog's chest twitched.

Ethan leaned closer. Shallow, ragged breaths now punctuated by small, ragged gasps. He pulled back, eyes scanning the fog, the empty fields. No one. No cameras. No witnesses.

He pressed again, tentative, fearing the touch might burn, and the warmth spread, fuller now, pulsing against the bones in his chest. It was alive. Too alive. Impossible alive.

The dog's eyes blinked open.

Ethan sank backward onto the roadside dirt, knees scraping, boots muddy, chest heaving. His hands trembled as the fog rolled in from the fields, curling over him, silent and accusing. He couldn't breathe. Couldn't think.

It was real. Not adrenaline. Not reflex. Not hallucination. Real.

Tears stung his eyes, unbidden. He blinked them away. Not here. Not like this. He could barely form the words in his mind: *I didn't... I didn't... I didn't do this. I didn't do this.*

And yet, he had. Somehow, impossibly, he had.

The dog stirred in his lap, weak but alive, licking at his hands with damp, shivering jaws. Ethan stared down at it. Close enough to smell the tang of blood, the wet musk of fur, the faint, unplaceable scent of life renewed.

Disbelief wrestled with awe, awe with panic.

He lifted the dog gently, cradling it against his chest. It was small, heavy in a way that reminded him of children in war zones, light and terrifying all at once. The fog didn't lift; it thickened, wrapping the world in silver silence.

Ethan's mind raced, searching for logic, an explanation. Maybe it had a faint pulse before he touched it. Maybe reflex. Maybe he'd imagined the warmth. Maybe, but deep down, he knew. *He knew.*

The truck started easily, the engine rumbling low beneath him. He drove home, hands shaking on the wheel, the dog tucked against his side. Silence filled the cab, broken only by the low, uneven panting of the little creature.

The truck hummed beneath him as he drove back toward the cabin. Each turn of the wheel felt like a decision he hadn't earned the right to make. The dog stayed pressed to his chest, breathing shallowly, eyes half-closed but alert. Ethan's hands shook despite his attempts to hold them steady. He wanted to believe it was adrenaline, the rush of panic, the lingering tension of combat. He wanted to believe this was all in his head. But every fiber of his body screamed that it wasn't.

The forested edges of his property rose like sentinels on either side of the gravel road. Fog lingered in the hollows, wrapping the trees in misty fingers. He had seen mornings like this before, quiet and eerie, but today it felt heavier. The air seemed to hum faintly, a vibration in his chest that he couldn't place. He glanced at the dog again. Its fur shimmered subtly in the low dawn light, and he swore he saw a faint glow, a pulse in its chest where he'd pressed his hands.

He shook his head, trying to dismiss it. He wasn't crazy. He wasn't hallucinating. Not this time.

By the time he reached the cabin, sweat had soaked through his shirt. He lifted the dog carefully, setting it on the rug in front of the stove. The little creature shook its body, muscles trembling as if waking from a dream. And then, it looked at him. Really looked at him. Eyes wide, intelligent, and unafraid. Not grateful. Not pleading. Just aware.

Ethan sank onto the floor beside it, leaning back against the wall. His mind ran in loops, memories of battlefield triage, failed resuscitations, faces he couldn't forget. In Afghanistan, he had carried men to safety only to watch some of them die anyway. Today, the dog had lived. Something inside him had made it live. And that something, he could feel it, was not entirely his own.

He pressed his palms against his knees, trying to steady the tremor in his chest. The room felt colder than it should, and the shadows in the corners seemed sharper, defined, almost alive. A faint warmth lingered in the air, like static electricity after a thunderstorm. He realized the dog's fur still shivered under his gaze, not from cold, but from something he couldn't name.

"What the hell..." he muttered under his breath, the words hollow in the quiet cabin.

He watched as the dog rose unsteadily to its feet, circling him once before settling by the stove. Each motion seemed deliberate, cautious, as if testing the boundaries of the life that had been restored. Ethan's stomach knotted. He had touched death and pulled it back and somewhere inside, he knew, if he could do this, what else could he do?

The thought made his chest tighten. Fear clawed at him. Not fear of death, he'd stared it down before, but fear of what he had become. Or perhaps, what had always been inside him, dormant, waiting for the right spark. The adrenaline faded, leaving a hollow, buzzing energy in its place. It settled in his bones, vibrating faintly, subtly, like a heartbeat not his own.

The dog's ears flicked at something behind him, and Ethan turned sharply. Nothing. Just the quiet creaking of the cabin settling in the cold morning air. He exhaled slowly, trying to convince himself it was over. But the feeling wouldn't leave. Something had changed. Something in the world had shifted and it had passed through him.

Hours slipped by. Ethan couldn't focus on chores, on breakfast, on the small, mundane tasks that had once grounded him. Every sound, every shadow, seemed heightened, sharper. He reached for a cup of coffee, hands still trembling. Steam rose in spirals from the mug, and for a brief moment, he imagined it twisting of its own accord, curling like smoke in impossible patterns. His heart slammed. He closed his eyes. Nothing. Just imagination. Just fear.

And yet.

He glanced at the dog again. It lay curled on the rug, breathing evenly. But even in sleep, its chest seemed to pulse faintly, glowing with a warmth that should not exist. Ethan's stomach lurched, a sickness born of awe and dread. He hadn't named it yet. Naming it would mean claiming responsibility. Acknowledging the impossible.

He didn't speak. He didn't move. He just stared. And in the quiet, with the fog creeping like a living thing outside the window, he understood something that both terrified and amazed him: life had passed through his hands, like water slipping over stones. Something primal, elemental, and utterly beyond him had obeyed.

The dog lifted its head. Its eyes met his. In them, Ethan thought he saw understanding. Not gratitude. Not fear. Not joy. But awareness. He shivered. The room seemed too still, the air too heavy. Somewhere, deep in the quiet, a faint hum pulsed. Not the wind. Not the house settling. Something else. Something waiting.

Ethan pressed his fingers against his forehead, unsure if he was checking for fever or if some instinct told him to mark himself against the unknown. The warmth from earlier lingered still, faint and humming under his skin. His chest ached, not from exertion, but from the weight of it, the weight of knowing that the world was wider, stranger, and more dangerous than he had ever allowed himself to believe.

Hours passed. The sun rose higher, cutting through the mist in thin, slanted shafts. Light spilled over the cabin floor, glinting off the dog's fur. And still, Ethan sat, rigid, eyes fixed on the creature. A knot of fear, disbelief, and awe twisted inside him. His mind refused to settle.

The dog shifted, padded closer, and lay its head in his lap. Warm. Real. Impossible.

Ethan's breath hitched. His hands, shaking from exhaustion, hovered over it. He did not dare touch it again. Not yet. Not until he understood what had happened.

And yet, he couldn't look away.

The quiet stretched, thick and suffocating, as the reality settled in. He had broken the boundary. He had reached into the space between life and death and returned. He had become something he did not understand. Something that could not be contained.

The dog blinked up at him, small chest rising and falling with the rhythm of impossible life, and Ethan Moore, veteran, medic, and solitary man, understood with a chill that the world would never feel ordinary again.

The first act of resurrection had been done. And somewhere deep in him, a tremor of something darker, older, and infinite, stirred awake.

He did not name the dog that day. But he knew he would have to. And when he did, the name would mark the moment that his quiet, ordered life ended and the touch of life, unstoppable and terrifying, began.

4

Strange Vibrations

The morning air pressed against Ethan's face with the chill of early spring, sharp and clean. He stepped outside the cabin, rubbing the sleep from his eyes, and froze. The dog was there, sitting stiffly near the edge of the porch, ears alert, chest rising and falling with quiet, measured breaths.

Ethan hadn't expected to see it again. Not like this. Hogan, he hadn't even named it yet, looked at him as though he belonged, as though he had been waiting all night. The sight twisted something inside him, a mixture of relief and unease that made his chest tight.

He closed the cabin door behind him, the lock clicking in the quiet. "You're still here," he said, almost whispering, but the sound felt strange, alien even. The dog's eyes flicked toward his, sharp, intelligent, unnervingly calm.

Ethan knelt slowly, careful not to startle it. "Alright," he muttered. "You can stay. For now." He exhaled, a long, shuddering breath, and finally whispered, "Hogan. You're Hogan now."

Hogan's ears twitched at the name. The dog tilted its head, curious, like it understood. Ethan found himself studying the animal as though it were a mirror, reflecting his own scarred solitude back at him. A reminder that life; fragile, messy, stubborn, persisted even here, in his tiny, isolated corner of Tennessee.

He rose and moved toward the barn, Hogan padding silently behind him. His hands itched, fingers curling as he reached for a hammer and nails. But the tingle in his palms had returned, faint, insistent, like static electricity beneath the skin. He paused, feeling the vibration deep in his bones. The hammer wobbled in his grip for no reason. A fleeting hum filled the air, soft but unmistakable.

Ethan shook his hands. "Get a grip," he muttered. Nothing moved, and the barn remained still. The hum vanished. Rational thought, always the savior. It had to be nerves, lingering from the night's storm, the wind, maybe a low-frequency tremor in the ground.

But Hogan was watching him. Not just watching, studying, waiting; and when Ethan dropped the hammer, it rattled on the floor in a rhythm that seemed almost... responsive.

He shook his head. "You're imagining it," he said aloud. He stepped outside and leaned against the railing, eyes on the creek that snaked lazily through the property. The water reflected the pale morning sun, ripples catching light in tiny, liquid diamonds. Hogan sat near the bank, ears forward, tail still. He didn't move except to glance at Ethan now and then.

Ethan exhaled slowly, trying to ground himself. He wanted normal. He wanted mundane. Morning chores. Feed the dog, repair the fence, work the land. But the tingling in his hands had a stubborn persistence, crawling like an itch he couldn't scratch. And every time he looked at Hogan, he felt it again, that quiet pull, the subtle weight of something more.

By noon, he had finished the repairs, but the unease followed. He sat on the porch, watching the creek, trying to ignore the small dissonances, the way the wind whispered through the trees, carrying patterns in its rhythm that seemed intentional, almost linguistic. A leaf twirled upward, spinning in a way that felt deliberate, as if marking a path. Hogan's eyes followed it. Ethan's heart thumped in response, rapid, shallow.

Night fell reluctantly, dragging shadows across the cabin. Ethan tried to eat, tried to read, tried to force himself into routines that had once grounded him. But sleep would not come, and when it did, it came with visions.

The first dream was of a woman. Golden-eyed, hair streaming like liquid bronze, skin luminous in the half-light. She floated above a vast sphere, threads of light weaving across the continents in patterns Ethan could almost understand but not name. Her voice was a whisper in a tongue he did not know, yet the meaning resonated like a memory: *"The seal is thinning."*

Ethan woke with a start, sheets tangled, heart hammering. The tingle in his hands returned, stronger now, pulsing beneath the skin like a living thing. Hogan lay at the foot of the bed, calm, watching him with unnerving stillness.

He rubbed his face with both hands. Rational thought clawed at him. *Adrenaline. Stress. You're alone. Nothing happened. Nothing.*

But the hum in the air lingered, faint, insistent. His hands shook slightly as he ran them over the mattress, feeling a warmth that had no source. Hogan shifted, almost nudging him, alert to something Ethan could not yet perceive.

Ethan sat on the edge of the bed, head in his hands, wrestling the terror that edged the awe. *What is happening?*

The creek murmured outside, a soft, liquid rhythm against the night. And in the shadows beyond the cabin, Ethan sensed it: subtle, alive, watching.

The tingle in his palms was a promise, and the golden-eyed woman's words echoed unbidden. *The seal is thinning.*

He looked down at Hogan, chest tight, eyes wide, trembling. *If this is real... what am I going to do?*

For the first time since he had found the dog, the line between fear and wonder blurred. And he did not know which would claim him first.

The next morning, Ethan woke to the soft insistence of dawn, light pooling like liquid across the cabin floor. Hogan lay curled at his feet, chest rising in a steady rhythm. The dog stirred when Ethan's fingers twitched, and for a brief, strange moment, it seemed aware, responsive to some unspoken cue he didn't understand.

Ethan rubbed his eyes, heart still rattling from the dream. *A dream,* he repeated to himself. *Nothing real.* Yet the warmth in his palms lingered, a residual pulse he could neither explain nor shake.

Breakfast was mechanical; eggs, toast, black coffee. He barely tasted it, mind circling the previous night. Every time he brushed his fingers over the mug, a soft vibration tickled his skin. He dropped it once, and the cup clattered to the floor, yet didn't shatter. Just skidded across the wood, landing upright on its edge. He froze, eyes wide, pulse surging. Hogan tilted his head, ears pricked, unafraid.

Ethan exhaled slowly, kneeling to lift the cup with hands that trembled. *You're imagining it. It's the nerves. Nothing else.*

Out the window, the creek outside ran unusually bright under the morning sun, sunlight scattering across the water in points of fire that seemed to dance toward him, not with the current but against it. He frowned, gripping the railing. *No. Stop reading too much into this.*

He stepped outside, Hogan padding silently at his heels, and allowed himself a slow survey of the land. The wind moved through the trees in uneven gusts, rattling the cabin siding in patterns that felt almost deliberate. Leaves twirled upward, circling each other briefly before drifting back down. It was subtle, almost invisible but Ethan felt it in the pit of his stomach, an unshakable certainty that something had changed.

Curiosity warred with fear. Tentatively, he reached for a fallen twig and held it between his fingers. The tingle ran through his palm, small but insistent. He flexed his fingers. The twig quivered, then rose a few inches, hovering for a breath before dropping.

Ethan jerked back, pulse pounding. Hogan barked, a sharp, alert sound, but did not move. Ethan's chest constricted. *This isn't real. It can't be real.*

But the moment of doubt was immediately replaced by wonder. The air felt thicker now, alive. He reached again, trembling, and touched a patch of grass. A single blade bent toward his palm, green brightening in an impossible flash. His breath hitched. He dropped to his knees, touching more grass no more flashes. The residual warmth in his hands spread, a steady thrum beneath his skin.

He leaned back against the porch railing, sweat prickling at his temples. *What is happening to me?*

The day wore on in a tense blur. Hogan followed him everywhere, silent and watchful. Every minor flicker of electronics, the flicker of a light bulb, the stutter of his laptop screen, made him flinch. He waved a hand too near the coffee maker, and it sputtered, steaming erratically before returning to normal.

By late afternoon, the tension had climbed to a nearly unbearable pitch. Ethan tried to work on repairs around the cabin, chopping wood, mending the fence. Each movement brought the same faint hum under his skin. The hammer vibrated unexpectedly in his hand, nails quivering as though alive. He threw it down, heart hammering. Hogan stayed at a careful distance, eyes alert, unblinking.

That night, sleep became impossible. Ethan lay in bed, sheets twisted around him, staring at the ceiling. Every shadow seemed to move with intent. He could feel the hum in the air now, low, almost imperceptible, but it pulsed in tandem with his own heartbeat. Hogan lay at the foot of the bed, unmoving, ears flicking at nothing he could hear.

Then it came, the vision, sharper than the first. The golden-eyed woman appeared again, floating above a sphere that pulsed like a living thing. Threads of light wrapped the globe in intricate patterns. She reached toward him, and the air shimmered as if her fingers brushed the room itself. A circle with 5 straight lines intersecting each with a rune at the end glowing blue, hovered in the air.

"The seal is thinning," she whispered, words vibrating with weight he could feel in his chest.

He bolted upright, gasping, palms glowing faintly in the dim light. Hogan stood immediately, hackles raised, eyes locked on Ethan's hands. The warmth coursing through him had not faded. The hum persisted, vibrating beneath his skin, connecting him to something vast and unseen.

Ethan's breaths came in ragged bursts. He touched the floorboards, the walls, even Hogan's fur, and felt the same pulse, the same life thrumming. *Am I... causing this?*

Hogan nuzzled his hand, calm but insistent. Ethan recoiled, torn between fear and awe. Each small pulse of energy left a mark on him, tiny sparks of light lingering briefly on surfaces, as if the world itself remembered the touch.

Hours passed like that, until the first faint light of dawn seeped through the cabin windows. Ethan hunched over on the edge of the bed, burying his face in his hands, Hogan leaning against him with measured patience. The hum receded, leaving a quiet resonance in the air that felt almost mournful, like the world exhaling after a storm.

He looked at the dog, heart tight, chest aching. *I don't understand any of this,* he admitted aloud, voice hoarse. The dog's eyes met his, steady and unafraid, and in that moment Ethan understood, in a gut-level way, that Hogan had been more than a spark. He had been the first proof.

The awe and terror collided in him, heavy, unrelenting. He felt the energy beneath his skin, pulsing, waiting. The dream, the warmth, the hum, it all pressed against him, and he could not look away. Hogan whined softly, nudging him, and Ethan realized that the dog was no longer just a dog. Not really.

He swallowed hard, feeling the weight of the realization settle deep into his bones. The world had shifted while he slept. The hum of life, the subtle glow of magic, it wasn't gone. It had found him.

And he had no idea how to stop it.

5

The Vet

The morning came gray and low, a thin mist curling along the edges of the road as Ethan drove into town toward the Vet's office. Hogan sat in the passenger seat, quiet, head resting on his paws, watching the world slide past. Ethan kept his hands tight on the wheel, his knuckles pale. Every mile felt longer than it should, each turn weighted with dread. He'd called to set up an appointment to have Hogan checked out. He'd explained he had found Hogan on the side of the road injured. Now he wondered if he should have.

The vet's office sat on a side street just off Main, an unassuming brick building with a faded sign swaying slightly in the wind. A bell chimed as he pushed open the door, and the sterile smell of antiseptic hit him like a wall. Hogan's paws clacked softly on the tile floor, and Ethan felt a tickle of unease. The dog hadn't hesitated, he had followed willingly, as though he understood that Ethan needed this more than he realized.

Inside, the waiting room was empty. Lila Anderson emerged from a side door, her white coat crisp, hair tied back, eyes sharp behind her glasses.

"Ethan, good morning." she said. Her voice was even, professional. There was no judgment in it, but Ethan felt every syllable settle over him like a weight. "Found another stray I see."

"Yes, ma'am" he said, keeping his tone flat. He didn't look at her, instead guiding Hogan into a corner where the dog lay quietly.

"I understand you found this one injured?" she asked, crouching slightly so she could examine Hogan at eye level. "We'll take a look."

Ethan nodded, stiff. He didn't speak, didn't elaborate. Not here. Not anywhere.

Hogan allowed her to check him, rolling onto his side, letting her run her hands along his limbs. She pressed on his paws, flexed joints, and palpated muscles, murmuring professional observations. Ethan watched, tense, heart thumping in his chest. Every time she touched him, Hogan remained calm, completely healed. The injuries, the broken bones, the shock of the roadside accident, they were gone.

"Nothing," she said finally, straightening. "No swelling. No abrasions. No bruising. He's perfect."

Ethan felt the air leave his chest. Perfect. The word echoed in his mind like a hammer against glass.

"That's... impossible," Lila said quietly, almost to herself. She glanced at Ethan, eyebrows knitting. "I've seen some odd recoveries in my time, but nothing like this. He should be..." She shook her head. "...he should still be hurt."

Ethan's stomach turned. He wanted to laugh, to curse, to tell her it was just luck, a miracle of adrenaline and chance, but the truth gnawed at him. He had felt it in his hands, the pulse, the warmth, the surge that had traveled from his chest into the dog. He had watched Hogan take a breath where before there had been none.

"Probably just... shock," Ethan said finally. His voice was rough, hoarse. "Adrenaline. Dogs have crazy resilience. You know how it is."

Lila studied him, skeptical but cautious. "Maybe," she said slowly. "But the timing... and the recovery... There's nothing natural about it."

Ethan swallowed, feeling a cold sweat gather at his hairline. He wanted to leave, to run, but he stayed, rooted by something he couldn't name. Hogan lifted his head, looking at him with calm, knowing eyes. The dog's gaze felt heavier than it should, as if he understood what Ethan could not admit even to himself.

The subtle hum began again, low and almost imperceptible, a vibration that threaded through the air and clung to the edges of Ethan's awareness. It came from him, he knew it, and yet it seemed to linger in the room itself, brushing against Lila's ankles, vibrating softly beneath the tiles. His stomach knotted, a mixture of awe and dread that he couldn't shake.

"I need to take him back for observation," Lila said finally. "Routine check-ups. I want to monitor him."

Ethan shook his head. "No, that's fine. We'll... we'll just go home. Thanks."

She raised an eyebrow but said nothing, clearly sensing the tension, the undercurrent of something she could not name. Hogan leaned into Ethan as he straightened, brushing against his legs. Ethan felt the warmth radiating through him again, faint, fleeting, a reminder of what had happened on the roadside.

Outside, the wind had picked up. Mist rolled along the asphalt, curling around parked cars, drifting between the buildings. Ethan kept his eyes on the road, hands tight on the wheel. He felt Hogan shift in the seat beside him, and the dog's quiet confidence contrasted sharply with the storm of thoughts in Ethan's mind.

At the edge of the forest that bordered his property, he stopped. Hogan jumped down, sniffing at the ground. Ethan watched him go, but the dog's behavior had changed. He moved with purpose now, alert, aware of something invisible threading through the air.

Ethan's hands tingled. A faint vibration traveled from his fingertips into his arms. He flexed his fingers, trying to shake off the sensation. The hum that had brushed against Lila's ankles inside the clinic now seemed contained, concentrated in his palms, like the residual heat after a fire. He clenched his fists, forcing it down, forcing it away, but the awareness of it left him drained, alert, and terrified.

He remembered the whispers in the wind from the night of the storm, the low calling of his name that had made sleep impossible. It wasn't just the wind. It wasn't just a dream. Something else had stirred that night, and now, in the light of day, with Hogan calm at his side, Ethan felt the first clear confirmation: the world was no longer ordinary, and neither was he.

At the cabin, he placed Hogan's leash on a hook by the door, then stood in the living room, staring at the dog. Every instinct told him to run, to bury himself in the solitude of his farm, but the dog remained, a quiet, steady presence that had come back from the brink of death.

Ethan touched the dog's fur lightly, half-expecting the warmth to vanish, half-expecting it to surge again. It was there. Solid, undeniable. Hogan nuzzled against him, a quiet acknowledgment of the bond formed in that terrifying, miraculous moment.

Ethan stepped back, shaking. The room felt smaller, more intimate, charged with something he couldn't explain. The ordinary life he had clung to, the routines, the discipline, the isolation, had begun to fracture. The hum in his hands lingered faintly, like an echo of a bell struck somewhere deep beneath the earth.

He thought of Lila, skeptical yet observant, and of the impossibility of Hogan's healing. He thought of the wind that had whispered his name. He thought of the storm that had passed and left the world unscarred, though somehow changed.

The dog looked up at him, eyes dark and intelligent, waiting.

And in that quiet, fragile moment, Ethan understood something he had never allowed himself to consider. He was not alone. Not in the world, and not in what was happening inside him.

Shaken, awed, terrified, he stared at Hogan, and the hum thrummed in the air once more, faint but persistent.

The cabin, the dog, the wind outside, they were all witnesses now, and there was no turning back.

6

Reverberations

Ethan rose before the sun, boots hitting the dew-slick grass with the quiet precision of someone used to moving through danger. The air smelled of wet earth and pine, but something else lingered beneath it, a metallic tang he couldn't name, a current under the skin of the land. Hogan padded close behind, nose to the ground, tail low, following Ethan with that unnerving patience that made the dog seem half aware of things Ethan wasn't ready to see.

The birds were the first to break the morning's fragile calm. At first, he thought it was coincidence, a murder of crows perhaps but as he reached the edge of the creek, they lifted in a dense, swirling cloud, shrieking with intensity. Not scattered flight. Not feeding. They rotated, a spiraling dance he could feel in his chest. Their calls pitched, modulated, like language he couldn't parse. The hair on his arms rose.

Ethan stopped. Hogan sat, ears pricked. The creek's water, silvered with the early sun, shivered unnaturally. Tiny waves rolled upstream against no current. He squinted. Was that light? Glinting, flickering, golden, just at the surface. He reached down, fingertips brushing the cold water. A subtle pulse traveled from the creek into his palms, a thrum he couldn't explain.

He yanked his hand back, breath shallow. "It's not real," he muttered, more to steady himself than to convince anyone. But the thrum stayed, lingering under his skin, a quiet insistence.

Hogan growled softly. Ethan's head snapped toward the dog. Nothing. Just the hum of the birds, the creek, the wind through the pines.

Later, inside his cabin, he set up his phone and camcorder on the table. If he could just catch it on video, birds, the creek, something, maybe he could convince himself this wasn't madness. He turned them on, watched the screens flicker.

The devices blinked, sputtered. Static raced across the camcorder, the phone froze. He shook the devices. On the camcorder, for a heartbeat, a faint symbol appeared: a circle with five lines branching from it. Just long enough to imprint itself on the corner of his eye. Then gone.

Ethan pressed the phone to his chest. His heartbeat roared in his ears. The hum came back, this time in his hands, low but unmistakable. He flexed fingers. A small shock, like a brush of static, jumped across his skin. Hogan whined.

He slammed the devices down. "I'm losing it," he whispered.

And maybe he was. But something told him that whatever this was, it wasn't going to wait for him to understand.

That night, he couldn't sleep. The hum never stopped. Outside, wind twisted through the trees, low and constant. He lay on the floor beside Hogan, staring at the ceiling, every nerve taut.

A voice, soft as rustling leaves, called his name. He sat up instantly. "Who's there?"

Nothing. Just the wind.

Then: the words came again, faint, foreign, melodic but clear, "*The circle frays.*"

Ethan's stomach sank. His hands shook. The air around him quivered, like it couldn't quite decide whether it wanted to stay or flee. He crawled to the creek, moonlight streaking across the cabin window. The water glimmered with a thin, golden light, tracing ripples that weren't caused by anything he could see.

Hogan moved forward, nose low to the surface. Ethan followed, heart hammering. The water rose slightly, shimmering, bending toward him as if acknowledging his presence. He dared not touch it, trembling, awed and afraid all at once.

Something ancient was stirring. Something alive. And it had found him.

Over the next few hours, exhaustion pulled him along in fits of frantic observation. He tested small movements, nudging a stone with his foot. It rolled unnaturally, spinning briefly before settling. A leaf on a nearby branch quivered, as though caught in an unseen current.

The hum grew stronger in his palms. A surge of warmth shot through him when he touched the creek again. For a moment, the air tasted electric, thick with possibility. Hogan sniffed the waves, tail low, patient. Ethan realized, with a shiver, that the dog might understand this in ways he didn't.

He pressed his palms to the water again. Light rippled outward, faint but unmistakable. He felt his chest tighten, not from effort but from recognition: this wasn't him doing something to the world. The world was doing something with him.

And the thought made his stomach churn.

By dawn, Ethan collapsed on a log, dripping sweat, knees pulled tight to his chest. Hogan sat beside him, eyes alert. The creek, now calm, still shimmered faintly, as though holding its breath.

He thought about what he had just done. About what had been happening for days. About the hum in his hands, the light in the creek, the birds, the voice. About what it might mean.

Responsibility. Power. Danger. Discovery.

His chest ached not from exertion but from the weight of understanding. He realized he could no longer ignore it. The Weave, the strange, living pulse in the world, had chosen him. And that choice came with consequences he wasn't ready to face.

Yet the hum remained, persistent, insistent, as if encouraging him forward.

Ethan turned toward the creek, tracing the faint ripples with his eyes. Hogan sat silently, calm. And for the first time, Ethan understood: nothing in his life would ever be the same again.

The sun climbed higher, but the light didn't feel ordinary. It was muted, like it had passed through a veil of water or smoke. Ethan moved along the creek's edge, Hogan at his heels, every step hesitant. He had tried to ignore the hum, tried to tell himself it was nothing more than exhaustion, adrenaline, or lingering trauma, but the pulse in his palms wouldn't let him.

A ripple ran across the creek, gentle at first. He knelt, letting his fingers brush the water. The ripple grew, coiling outward like a snake, then leapt up into the air, freezing in a golden arc before dissipating into mist. Hogan barked once, low and urgent. Ethan drew back, his breath hitching. He felt it in his chest first, then in his fingertips: a resonance he had never known, a heartbeat larger than his own.

He lifted a fallen branch. It floated briefly, suspended midair. Gravity seemed to hesitate before tugging it down. His stomach churned, disbelief clashing with awe. *I'm not doing this,* he told himself. *It's not me. This isn't me.*

Yet every movement, every heartbeat, made the creek and the surrounding air respond. Leaves swirled around him without wind. Tiny motes of light danced over the water. Hogan crouched, tail low, sniffing at the shimmering edge of the creek. It was as though the dog understood the pulse, recognized it as part of the world rather than a threat.

Ethan backed away, hands trembling. He closed his eyes, willing himself to think rationally, to convince himself he was seeing things. But when he opened them, the water had risen slightly, rippling outward as if acknowledging him. And he was certain now that the hum wasn't just in his palms, it was in his chest, threading through his bones, the rhythm of something larger.

He picked up a rock, rolling it between his fingers. The hum amplified. He tossed it into the creek. It didn't sink immediately. It hovered for a moment, then skimmed along the surface like a skipping stone animated by invisible energy. Ethan staggered back. Hogan's bark echoed in the trees, sharp and insistent.

"What are you doing?" Ethan whispered to himself, voice raw. "What the hell is happening?"

The birds returned, black shapes spiraling overhead. They circled faster this time, a tornado of wings, screeching in a cadence that matched the hum threading through Ethan's body. Every nerve in him screamed. The creek glowed brighter, a thin, golden line tracing the edges of the bank, moving like ink in water.

Ethan sank to his knees, trying to ground himself. He pressed his palms to the mud. The pulse responded instantly. Vibrations ran up his arms, then down his spine, and for a moment the world felt hollow, like a bell about to ring. He pulled his hands away, gasping.

I am not imagining this.

Hogan stepped closer, nuzzling Ethan's side. The dog's warmth, his steady presence, tethered him just enough. But the wonder and fear collided, an impossible mixture he could neither reconcile nor resist.

He spent the next hour testing, experimenting quietly, cautiously. A fallen leaf spun in his palm. A broken twig reassembled itself before snapping apart again. A patch of grass that had wilted under the morning sun shot upward, green and glistening, as though freshly painted.

Every act drained him. Every act left a small ache in his chest, a flutter of nausea. The hum followed him like a shadow, never ceasing, growing louder whenever he tried to focus. And still, the creek responded.

At one point, he pressed a hand flat against the water's surface, and the creek's glow pulsed in concentric circles. Hogan lay down beside him, head resting on his leg, calm in a way that made Ethan's panic spike. The dog seemed to know that what he was doing was bigger than either of them.

The sun moved, shadows stretching and folding across the property. Ethan's hands shook as he pulled back from the water. His mind raced: *What if this is permanent? What if I can't stop it?*

He thought of the dreams, the voice of the golden-eyed woman, her words ringing in his head: *The circle frays.*

He didn't understand what she meant. He didn't want to. And yet, he couldn't ignore it.

As evening fell, the manifestations became more insistent. A sudden wind whipped through the trees, bending branches without a breeze. Hogan growled, low in his throat. Ethan's hair lifted along his arms. Tiny sparks of light arced between rocks at the creek's edge.

He touched the water again. It responded instantly, swelling up to his wrists, shimmering with molten gold. His chest constricted. Fear, awe, exhaustion, and exhilaration collided inside him, and he stumbled backward. The glowing creek receded slowly, reluctantly, as if it were bound to his presence but had its own will.

Ethan collapsed to the ground, eyes wide. The hum in his hands had turned into a roar inside his skull. Hogan pressed close, a living anchor in the chaos. Ethan's gaze returned to the creek. Golden light, faint but unmistakable, traced ripples across the surface.

His mind teetered on the edge of understanding. Whatever this was, whatever he had become a part of it was bigger than him. Larger than anything he had faced in Afghanistan, larger than anything in his life. And it was responding to him.

The wind whispered again, not his name this time, but a single word: *See.*

Ethan's chest ached. He reached forward with trembling fingers. The water shimmered, lifting slightly to meet him halfway, like a mirror of intent. Hogan's eyes gleamed in the dim light, fixed on the creek. And for the first time, Ethan didn't flinch.

He stared, awed, terrified, and utterly certain that his life had changed forever.

The world was alive, listening, waiting. And it had found him.

7

The Boy in the Lake

The morning was brittle and sharp, sunlight slicing through the trees in narrow beams. Ethan tightened the straps on his boots, the leather creaking under the small weight of routine, and Hogan pressed close at his side, tail swishing in short, anxious beats. They moved in silence down the narrow dirt path toward the reservoir, the air cool and sweet with the smell of water and earth. The world was quiet, but it hummed under the surface. Ethan felt it in the vibration of the ground beneath his boots, in the way the birds circled above, watching, whispering.

He kept his eyes on the path. Every instinct warned him to scan for movement, for danger. The past lingered just beneath the surface: dust clouds rising under distant gunfire, the snap of a twig that could mean death, screams caught in wind that carried bodies away. The old reflexes lingered, but the world was peaceful here, quiet enough to trick him into thinking it safe.

Hogan tugged at his leash, growling softly, ears pinned forward. Ethan's gaze followed the dog's alert posture. There, near the edge of the reservoir, a flash of motion. A boy. Too small. Struggling. Panicked.

Ethan's stomach dropped. The child flailed, legs kicking blindly, and water rushed into his mouth. Hogan barked once, urgent, and

Ethan dropped the leash, running. His boots sank into the soft mud, water spattering up, soaking the hem of his pants.

"Hey! Get to shore! Hold on!" Ethan shouted, voice cracking with raw instinct. The boy's head dipped under again. Time slowed, the world narrowing to that single, screaming pulse of life under threat. He dove.

The water shocked him, cold and unyielding, clawing at his chest and lungs. He felt the mud tug at his fingers as he swam, his arms carving through the chill. The boy's tiny hands grasped blindly at the water, at nothing, at him. Ethan seized him, lifting him into the surface. The child was limp, eyes closed, lips turning a sickly blue.

He hit the edge of the water, hauled the boy onto the bank. "Come on," Ethan muttered through clenched teeth, checking for breathing, pulse, anything. Nothing. Just cold, silent resistance. His hands pressed to the boy's chest. He gave the first breaths, counting. One, two... nothing.

A faint hum prickled across Ethan's skin, faintly electric. He recoiled for a heartbeat, then pressed on. The warmth began in his chest, radiating outward, along his arms and into his hands. He felt it move, a current unlike anything he'd known, pulling the boy into him, into life.

And then the boy gasped.

Air rushed into his lungs like wind into sails, and he coughed, coughing up the water, crying, wailing. Ethan dropped to the muddy bank, hands trembling, heart hammering, sweat and water mingling on his forehead. He looked down at the boy, alive, breathing, his small chest rising and falling, and his own mind refused to process it.

Hogan pressed close, tail stiff, whining softly. Ethan could feel residual energy pulsing along his fingers, tingling in the air, disturbing the leaves. He glanced up. A couple of bystanders had drawn closer, phones raised, faces pale and wide-eyed.

"What the hell, ?" one whispered.

Ethan scrambled to his feet, eyes darting, searching. There were more people now, emerging from the trees. Murmurs swelled into shocked chatter, and the clicking of cameras and phones rang sharp in the morning air. The quiet shoreline he'd trusted, the small pocket of control he'd clung to, vanished.

He backed away, glancing at Hogan, at the boy now attended by frantic parents and emergency personnel. The boy's mother hugged him, sobbing, but Ethan couldn't hear their words. All he could hear was the hum, faint but insistent, still pulsing along his skin and through the air around him.

Panic crawled up his spine. The realization struck him full: they had seen it. Recorded it. It would spread. The quiet life he had built, the careful walls he had set around himself, they were gone.

He stumbled backward, boots sliding on the damp earth, mud coating his hands. Hogan pressed against him, nudging, protective, anxious. Ethan's chest rose and fell rapidly. He swallowed hard, tasting copper and fear. The residue of the power lingered, the soft burn of something unnatural in his veins.

He turned, running. Away from the reservoir, away from the witnesses, the phones, the world that had just intruded on his life. The underbrush snagged at his pants; branches whipped his face. Hogan ran alongside, panting, eyes alert. Ethan's mind raced, images of what just happened collided with memories he didn't want to face: medics failing, soldiers dying, bodies slipping away, hands empty. He had touched life and brought it back. And he couldn't undo it.

By the time he reached the small path leading to the cabin, sweat and mud coated him, and his hands shook violently. He leaned against the door frame, drawing in deep breaths. Hogan nudged him again, calm now, sitting obediently.

Ethan stared down at the dog, who tilted his head, tongue lolling, ears perked. Hogan seemed... aware. Something in his gaze was uncomfortably intelligent. The hum had faded slightly, but the lingering weight of it pressed against Ethan's chest. He couldn't name it. Couldn't understand it. Only feel it.

He sank to the floor, back against the wall, and let his forehead rest on his knees. Hogan pressed against him, warm and living. The power had left a residue, a mark that wasn't visible, but was undeniable. Ethan's mind raced with questions he didn't want to answer: *What am I? What just happened? What happens if it happens again?*

Outside, the wind shifted, brushing across the property. A single leaf spiraled down from the old oak near the creek, landing softly on the porch. Ethan stared at it, and the hairs on his arms lifted. The world wasn't quiet anymore. Something had changed.

He closed his eyes, breathing ragged, listening to the faint, residual hum under his skin, and felt the weight of what he'd just done. Heroism and horror tangled into something that left him raw, hollow, and utterly awake.

When he looked down at Hogan, the dog's dark eyes meeting his, Ethan's chest tightened. There was awe there, and fear. A recognition of power he could not yet name, cannot yet control. And he knew, deep in his gut, that the day's events had broken the fragile barrier he had built around his life.

Something had shifted. Something had begun.

8

Firestorm

The television glared in the corner, a cold light that refused to relent. Ethan sat on the edge of the sofa, shoulders hunched, eyes fixed yet not seeing. The looped footage from the lake rolled endlessly: him diving, the boy flailing, the surge of light across his hands. "Miracle Medic Rescues Drowning Child in Tennessee, Witnesses Stunned," the banner screamed.

He didn't move. Hogan's paws scraped softly against the floor as the dog circled him, then settled beside his boots. The cabin smelled faintly of damp wood and old coffee. The quiet was unbearable. Even with the sound of the television, Ethan felt hollow, like the world had collapsed inward.

Online, it was chaos. Clips of shaky cellphone recordings stacked atop each other: angles from witnesses, the boy gasping, Ethan's hands faintly glowing blue. Tweets ran past on a ribbon of light: *"That's not possible!"* *"The energy field, what is happening?"* *"He's got to be a threat."* Notifications pinged, some vibrating against the wooden table. He ignored them. Ignoring didn't help. Every vibration felt like a hammer striking against his ribs.

He remembered the lake. The feel of the boy's weight, the surge of energy moving through him, and the blue rune burning faintly across his hands. That surge had not left him. It pulsed somewhere in the marrow of his bones, a quiet heartbeat that refused to stop.

Then the knocks began. Soft at first, almost hesitant. Tap, tap, tap. A few minutes later, louder, pounding: reporters at the end of his gravel drive, shouting into megaphones, cameras flashing like the sun. Drones buzzed overhead, circling. He sank to the floor, pressing his back to the wall. Hogan stayed close, nose twitching, ears forward.

He remembered a firefight in Afghanistan, a similar sound, the whine of incoming rounds, the pounding in his chest. But this wasn't bullets. This was curiosity, fear, fascination. A thousand invisible eyes trained on him.

Goddamn it, he thought, gripping the floorboards. *Just leave me alone.*

Through the walls, the hum began, faint at first, then insistent. Lights flickered. The television's glow pulsed. Even Hogan's fur seemed to shimmer. Ethan's chest tightened. Hands curling into fists, he flexed, tried to ground himself. The warmth in his palms throbbed, the faint pulse lingering like a warning.

On the screen, social media feeds were exploding. Comments scrolled faster than he could read. Clips of bystanders zoomed in on his hands. "Look at the glow!" "Miracle or hoax?" "He's dangerous!" Every word chipped at him, reminding him that there was no hiding.

He thought of the boy, gasping, the blue rune flashing. That moment, the surge, was no longer private. He was exposed. Vulnerable.

The knocks turned into banging. He could hear someone yelling, "Miracle Medic! Please, just talk to us!" It was hours before the sun dipped below the ridge, shadows stretching long across the cabin floor. Ethan's pulse quickened. Each light flicker, each hum, each vibration in his hands felt like an accusation.

Hogan growled low in his throat. Ethan scratched behind the dog's ears without thinking, grounding himself. *At least he doesn't panic,* Ethan thought, a bitter, fleeting thought. Hogan's calm presence was all he had.

Another hum, higher now, insistent, threading through the walls. The cabin seemed aware, reacting to him. Lights flickered again. A chair scraped across the floor as he shifted. The television went static for a heartbeat, then returned, distorted images overlaying the feed. He pressed his hands to his head, shaking. *I can't do this. I can't...*

Memories came unbidden: mortar fire, screams, the smell of burning metal. A man screaming for help, pinned under debris. He remembered lifting him, hands steady despite everything, carrying him away. But here, no one was pinned under rubble. The weight pressing down wasn't life, it was expectation.

He pressed his hands to the floor, the warmth surging through him. Hogan nuzzled his side. Ethan felt it, the faint shimmer again. Light pulsed along the edges of the walls, faint as breath, as though the air itself were alive. A rhythm aligned with his own pulse.

Outside, the media frenzy had grown. Drones hummed overhead. Cars idled on the gravel drive, reporters shouting, cameras rolling. Online, clips went viral: television shows dissecting the footage, conspiracy theories blooming. "Miracle Medic", the world had a name for him now.

The sound of the front door creaking open froze him. A shadow filled the doorway, human-sized, unmistakable. Lila. Dr. Lila Anderson, the town vet, the one who had examined Hogan, now standing on his porch, face drawn but resolute.

"Ethan," she called softly. "You can't hide anymore."

He didn't answer. The hum pulsed stronger, brushing against his skin, pressing into his chest. Hogan growled, a warning tone low in his throat.

"I saw the footage," Lila said, stepping closer, boots crunching on the floorboards. "I know it's real. I... I don't know what to think, you saved him."

Ethan's hands twitched. The warmth spread, faintly blue, brushing along his fingertips. "I..." he started, voice catching. He swallowed hard, but the words dissolved into nothing.

"Ethan," she said, voice steadier now, softer. "I'm not afraid of you." Her eyes searched his, a mix of fear and compassion. "But you need to control this... whatever it is."

He sank lower against the wall, pressing his palms into the floor as warmth pulsed in reply. The flickering light along the walls stretched higher, shadows shifting like liquid. His breath came in shallow gasps. "I can't," he said finally. "I don't know if I can."

She crouched beside him, placing a hand on his shoulder. The touch didn't startle him, though it hummed faintly in the hair of his arms. Hogan pressed close against her side, tail wagging slightly. "You're not alone," she said. "We'll figure it out."

The hum inside the cabin grew louder, vibrating through the floorboards, threading through Ethan's ribs. He felt it in his teeth, in the back of his skull, in his chest. Something else joined it, a whisper, subtle at first, curling around the edges of perception. *Ethan... Ethan...*

He froze. Breath caught. The name was not from outside. Not from the reporters. Not from the drones. It was closer, intimate, almost within him. A word carried on the current of the hum.

Hogan's ears twitched. The dog rose, alert. Ethan's hands tingled, warmth spreading, fingers curling as if the air itself were alive. The room pulsed with faint light. The walls shimmered along the grain of the wood. Shadows shifted like liquid.

Ethan sank to the floor, knees drawn up, forehead pressed to his arms. The hum intertwined with his heartbeat. The flickering glow along the walls stretched higher, tracing the grain of the ceiling. He reached a hand toward it, and the light pulsed brighter, a wave of warmth rolling through him. Hogan sat by his side, silent, watching.

Outside, the world raged: helicopters, cameras, tweets, livestreams. Inside, Ethan, Lila and Hogan sat in the quiet chaos of their own making. The hum continued, rhythmic, persistent. A pulse, a heartbeat, threading through the cabin and through him.

And in the midst of it, Ethan realized something profound and terrifying: the Weave was not done. It had found him. It pulsed in the walls, in the creek beyond, in the dog at his feet, and most of all, in his own blood.

He leaned back against the wall, hands trembling, eyes fixed on the faint shimmer of the supernatural flicker. Hogan rested his head on his paw. Ethan didn't speak. There were no words for what he felt. Awe. Terror. Responsibility. And beneath it all, the undeniable truth: nothing would ever be quiet again.

The cabin was still, but alive. And so was he.

The hum lingered, a quiet echo of the Weave, threading its way into every corner of his life.

9

The Preacher

The cabin felt impossibly quiet after Lila left. Ethan stood at the edge of the porch, watching the dust swirl along the gravel road as her truck disappeared behind the bend. Hogan stood at his feet, tail low but steady, the dog's presence grounding him.

The creek gurgled softly behind the house, its gentle rush like a heartbeat in the empty space. Ethan's own pulse thrummed with a residual tension he couldn't shake. The events of the day kept replaying in loops behind his eyes, the boy in the lake, the way the blue rune had flickered across his skin, the helpless faces of the witnesses frozen in astonishment. He'd tried to keep moving, tried to focus on small chores around the cabin, but every glance down at Hogan reminded him of what had happened. What he had done. And the unspoken truth that he hadn't asked for any of it.

He leaned on the railing, resting on his elbows, and let the wind brush his face. It whispered through the trees, carrying a faint, inexplicable cadence. He shook his head, hoping it was just the creek's reflection, the rustle of the leaves. Hogan nudged him gently, breaking the spiral of thought, and Ethan felt a brief tether to the ordinary, to something he could still call home.

The truck's engine cut through the quiet, rough against the soft hum of the creek. A figure stepped onto the drive, tall and lean, a familiar set of shoulders and the careful gait of someone who'd walked through fire and come out different. Samuel Tate.

Ethan stiffened. It had been years since Afghanistan, since they'd moved in sync under a shared threat, until the war had scattered them like leaves in a storm. Tate's hair had thinned and grayed, he wore a preacher's collar now and there was a steadiness in the man, a calm that always seemed to radiate outward even when the world was falling apart. Hogan growled softly, wary but not hostile, and Tate's hand rose in a slow, reassuring gesture.

"Ethan," Tate said, voice even, carrying the weight of old camaraderie. "Mind if I come in?"

Ethan's lips pressed together. He wanted to say no. Wanted to retreat behind the walls he had built around his cabin, around himself. But he nodded. "Yeah. Come in."

Inside, Tate's presence filled the room like sunlight breaking through a cloudy sky. He didn't sit immediately; he leaned against the doorframe, eyes scanning the small space, taking in the scattered papers, Hogan's careful pacing, the faint blue glow lingering in Ethan's palms.

"I've been following it," Tate said finally. "The footage, the news... your little miracle."

Ethan's stomach twisted. He looked away, to the creek outside, to the light slanting through the windows, and then back at Tate. "It wasn't... I don't know what it was."

Tate stepped closer, careful but purposeful. "You know what it was, Ethan. You know you did something. Something... extraordinary." His eyes softened. "God works in strange ways, my friend. Sometimes He chooses the least likely among us."

Ethan laughed dryly, a bitter, hollow sound. "God wouldn't pick someone like me."

Tate didn't flinch. "That's exactly why He might." He gestured to the faint flicker of blue light in Ethan's hands, subtle but undeniable.

"Power like yours doesn't show up in the ordinary. It doesn't happen to men who are at peace with themselves."

Ethan sank into the couch, rubbing his face with one hand. Hogan rested beside him, head on Ethan's knee, as if sensing the storm of guilt and disbelief thrumming through the room. "I've let men die I was supposed to protect," Ethan said, voice low, almost strangled. "I've failed them over and over. You think God cares about someone like me? I don't even care about me half the time."

Tate crouched to meet his eyes, not judgmental, only firm. "Caring isn't what this is about. What you've been given... it's not about comfort. It's about responsibility. You can't run from it."

Ethan shook his head, bitter, frustrated. "I'm not running. I'm surviving. That's all I can do."

Outside, the wind rustled through the trees, carrying with it a faint cadence that sent shivers across Ethan's skin. It was almost as if the creek itself was whispering, echoing Tate's words, or perhaps warning him. He clenched his fists; the faint blue pulse hummed again, a subtle vibration through his veins that left his chest tight.

Tate straightened, giving him space but holding Ethan's gaze. "Extraordinary things demand extraordinary courage. You think you're cursed. You think it's a burden. Maybe it is. But that doesn't change what's been done, or what will be done if you ignore it."

Ethan turned his eyes to the floor, to the dull gleam of sunlight catching dust motes. "I'm not... I'm not the man who can do this," he whispered.

"You don't have to be," Tate said quietly. "You only have to try. That's all anyone ever asks. That's all God asks. That's all life asks."

Hogan lifted his head, sensing the tension, and let out a soft whine. Ethan reached down, fingers brushing the dog's fur, grounding himself. Tate watched silently, understanding the tiny, human gestures that still tethered Ethan to the world.

Hours seemed to pass in silence. The hum in Ethan's hands lingered, subtle and rhythmic, as if measuring the beat of his own heart against something far larger. He thought of the boy in the lake, the viral footage, the flood of voices and eyes watching him without knowing him. He thought of the miracle he had unwillingly performed, the power he had barely begun to understand, and the moral weight pressing down inescapably.

Tate's hand rested briefly on his shoulder. "You're not alone, Ethan. Not this time."

Ethan wanted to argue, to reject, to retreat into isolation. But he found himself nodding, faintly, almost imperceptibly. He didn't trust the feeling. Didn't trust the calm that tried to settle over him. And yet... it lingered, a tiny spark of something he hadn't felt in years.

When Tate finally left, the cabin seemed suddenly larger, quieter, but heavy with the weight of unsaid things. Ethan moved to the creek outside, the water reflecting the late afternoon sky. His hands hovered just above the surface, the faint blue pulse lingering, almost imperceptible, but real. Hogan sat beside him, head down, eyes alert.

The whisper in the wind grew louder, clearer, or perhaps his mind filled in the pattern: *"The seal is thinning..."*

Ethan swallowed hard. The weight of what he had done, what he might do, pressed on him. He was shaken, awed, terrified. And somewhere deep inside, he knew, without understanding how, that his life had changed forever.

The creek ran quietly, serene, but it was not the same. And neither was he.

10

Agents

The television flickered again, casting a pale, stuttering light across the cabin's walls. Ethan didn't look at it directly. He could hear the faint drone of talking heads, some science, some speculation, some outright panic. "Miracle Medic," they said. Clips repeated in endless loops: the boy's chest rising and falling, Ethan's hands glowing faintly in the morning sun. Social media didn't just spread the story. It devoured it, shredded it, and regurgitated it in every imaginable form. Ethan stayed in the corner of the kitchen, Hogan at his feet, ears pricked, watching the shadows. The hum in the room had changed; it wasn't the static of the TV alone. There was something else, vibrating through the walls and the air.

He hadn't meant for any of this. The lake, the boy, the fleeting pulse of life, it had been instinct. A reflex. And now it had grown teeth.

By mid-morning, a black SUV rolled slowly down the dirt lane leading to the cabin. Ethan didn't hear it at first, but Hogan did. The dog stiffened, low growl rumbling in his chest. Ethan crouched, moving toward the front window. He saw the figure step out: tall, lean, posture controlled, eyes sharp behind sunglasses. The man carried a folder that looked too thick to be casual, and a badge glinted briefly in the sun. Agent Cole Ramirez.

Ethan's stomach clenched. This wasn't a rumor or an urban legend; it was real. Someone had decided he was worth tracking. The hum in his chest grew stronger, almost painful. Hogan whined softly at his side, pressing against his leg. Ethan tried to breathe through it, tried to remind himself that he could be anywhere, anyone could be mistaken, but the pulse of dread wouldn't abate.

Ramirez stepped closer, glancing up at the cabin as if he knew what to expect. The agent's movements were methodical, deliberate, and calm in a way that made Ethan's blood run faster. Surveillance footage, social media posts, and a dozen witness reports had been fed to him already. Ramirez had pieced together the timeline: the boy, the dog, the glowing hands, the inexplicable rise from death. Ethan hadn't meant to be seen. He hadn't meant to be noticed at all.

He tried to ignore the swelling pressure in his chest, tried to focus on Hogan, who moved restlessly beside him. And then it happened. The first small flicker. The lamps on the counter, battery-operated, shivered and dimmed. The old radio on the shelf squealed, then went dead. Ethan's heart pounded, not from fear, at first but from the awareness of the thing stirring inside him. Something in the air was charged, and it wasn't electricity alone.

Ramirez circled the property slowly. Ethan watched him like a hawk, counting the steps, noting the angle of the sun, the way the man's eyes scanned the treeline. The cabin felt smaller now, tighter, every shadow a potential threat. Hogan barked, and for a moment, Ethan panicked. What if the dog's instincts drew the agent closer? What if this exposure ended everything?

The lights flickered again. A faint blue shimmer played across Ethan's knuckles, barely noticeable but enough to make his throat dry. He flexed his hands, willing the pulse to stop, willing it back into nothing. But control was slipping. Just a little. And that little was terrifying.

Inside, Ethan tried to focus on normality. The kitchen smelled faintly of the coffee he hadn't drunk. The sunlight slanted across the counter in a way that made the dust motes dance like tiny specters. His breathing was uneven, chest tight, but he tried to ground himself: one step at a time. Hogan whined again, circling, pressing against him. Ethan's pulse throbbed in response, the hum rising. He could feel it, the strange resonance that had first manifested with the dog and then again at the lake. It was alive.

And it didn't care about him.

Ramirez didn't wait. He tapped on the cabin door lightly. One, two, three measured knocks. The sound reverberated in Ethan's chest like a bell. He froze, staring at the wood, feeling a wash of heat pulse through his veins. Hogan barked, snapping Ethan from his trance. He backed against the wall, calculating: could he escape through the back? Could he outrun a man like Ramirez? Could he fight what he didn't understand himself?

He swallowed, trying to calm the tremor in his hands. Small sparks danced along the edge of the countertop. The hum rose into a vibration that thrummed through the floorboards and into his bones. And still, he did nothing but watch.

The agent's voice came then, calm, precise, cutting through the thickening air. "Ethan Moore. We know you're in there. We just want to talk. No one has to get hurt."

Ethan's stomach dropped. Talk. That meant negotiation. That meant control. That meant exposure. His instincts screamed, and his body reacted before his mind could reason. Lights flickered. The old ceiling fan shuddered violently. Hogan barked, the sound sharp and frantic. The hum in Ethan's chest flared, brighter, stronger, and then, briefly, a shimmer of the creek water at the edge of the property seemed to rise, curling toward the cabin like a silver mist.

He stepped back, leaning against the wall. Control was thinning. The pulse in his hands, the hum in the air, the subtle glow at the edge of his vision, it all demanded attention, but Ethan refused. He couldn't afford to show power. Not yet. Not like this.

Hogan nudged his leg again, insistent, grounding. Ethan pressed his hands to his face, breathed in, tried to steady. Memories of the lake flooded back, the boy, the blue glow, the awe of life restored. And then the panic: what if he could never stop it? What if every heartbeat carried this dangerous pulse, this unwanted notice, this signal that screamed for attention?

Ramirez didn't move. The agent knew patience was a weapon. Ethan felt it. Felt the weight of being watched, calculated, hunted. Every instinct screamed at him to bolt. Every rational thought argued to stay hidden. The pulse in his hands grew sharper, tingling down his arms. Small objects shivered, utensils, a mug, the keys on the counter. He tried to focus, to will it back into inertia.

Nothing worked.

The sun shifted in the sky. Shadows lengthened. Ramirez's presence remained, unwavering. The agent wasn't just here to investigate; he was here to contain. Ethan could feel it, see it in the way the man moved, how the black SUV waited like a predator at the edge of the lane. Hogan's growl rose into a series of sharp barks.

And then the air cracked. A branch snapped underfoot, a bird shrieked. The hum surged through Ethan, now undeniable. A faint blue pulse flickered across his skin, his chest, hands, throat. The creek shimmered faintly in response, reflecting light in impossible angles. Ethan staggered back, mouth dry, heart pounding, eyes wide.

He had felt this before. At the lake. With the dog. But now it was different. Public. Observed. Uncontained. And it would not stop.

Hours passed in a blur. Ethan remained inside, barricading doors, listening to every sound outside: tires crunching gravel, distant voices, the faint echo of Ramirez's calculated steps. Hogan remained close, bristling, alert. Ethan flexed his fingers experimentally, willing the pulse to stop. A drawer rattled, a lamp flickered violently, the small hum in the floor thrummed like a warning.

He couldn't hide from it. Couldn't contain it. Couldn't even name it. All he could do was wait, listen, and feel the pulse of life, or something beyond life, coursing through him, aware, insistent, unstoppable.

By evening, the wind had picked up. The sky bruised with heavy clouds. Ethan's breaths came short, rapid. He stood near the creek, looking out at the reflective surface. The water was calm, almost serene, but in its depths, the faintest blue shimmer twisted and pulsed, responding to his heartbeat. Hogan nudged his leg again, low and insistent. Ethan's hands glowed faintly, fingers tingling, the hum now almost a voice in his skull.

And then he understood: nothing would be normal again. Not the world, not him, not Hogan, not the quiet farm. The creek, the dog, the pulse in his chest, it was all connected, and the first thread had already been pulled.

Ethan stared at the shimmer, the faint echo of the Weave in the air, and shivered. Fear, awe, and a strange, trembling wonder coiled in him. Somewhere beyond the trees, Ramirez watched, waiting, unaware of how close he was to something he could never comprehend.

Hogan licked Ethan's hand. The pulse lingered, faint but undeniable, thrumming in tandem with the dog's heartbeat. Ethan exhaled, trembling, and whispered into the dimming light:

"I didn't ask for this."

The creek reflected the sky, but something else moved in the water now, a subtle distortion, a shimmer, a reminder that life, power, and danger had returned, and there was no turning back.

11

Whispers in the Wire

Ethan watched the dust swirl along the edge of the gravel road as Agent Ramirez's sedan disappeared over the rise. The relief was almost physical, like the pressure in his chest had lifted, but only for a heartbeat. The hum in his ears didn't stop, and the residual tension in his hands reminded him that the world outside had already taken notice. They had seen him. Footage, witnesses. They were coming back.

The cabin was silent except for Hogan's low rumble behind the sofa. Ethan set the duffel bag down on the counter, running his hands over the worn fabric, still damp from the morning dew. He had always been a fixer, a man who could mend broken bodies, broken machines, broken systems. But nothing in his life had prepared him for this: a sickness in the world that didn't belong, threading through him, beyond him.

He slid the laptop toward him and hesitated. Screens flickered on the first tap of the power button, as if they had been waiting for him. The machine whined softly, the cooling fans shivering. He tapped keys methodically, searching military databases, old case studies, anything that might explain the impossible. Nothing fit. There was no precedent, no logic, no map.

And then the first anomaly appeared.

Lines of text blurred, words stretching and twisting. A folder he hadn't touched opened and closed. The glow of the screen shifted, like liquid light pooling into the center of the display. He leaned closer. The symbols that had haunted his dreams, the circle with five lines radiating outward, each tipped with a rune, pulsed faintly in the glow. His pulse raced.

It was subtle at first. A hair on his forearm lifted. A shiver traced down his spine. Hogan shifted, ears flicking. Ethan's hands tingled, the energy like a low vibration threading through his bones, familiar yet alien.

Then came the voice.

Static at first, like a whisper curling through the speakers, barely audible over the hum of the laptop. Ethan pressed his hands to his ears, thinking it might be a glitch. But the words broke through, fragile and deliberate: "Five... Hands..."

He recoiled, heart hammering. Not a dream. Not a hallucination. The static shifted, and he could almost make out the syllables, reverberating in the chest of his ribcage. He stared at the pulsing symbol on the screen, the circle spinning faintly, the runes glowing as if breathing.

Ethan's fingers hovered over the keyboard, trembling. He reached out tentatively, touching the glow. The hum surged, a pulse that coiled up his arms and back into his chest. The hairs on his arms stood rigid; the energy was alive. Alive, and responding.

Hogan whined softly, nudging against his leg. Ethan's head snapped down. The dog's eyes reflected the symbol on the screen, unblinking, almost knowing. The room felt like it had expanded, the walls breathing, the air thick with pressure.

He tried to document it. Pressed record. The files corrupted instantly. Every attempt to capture the phenomenon failed, rewinding, freezing, or dissolving into static. And still, the hum remained, threading through him, urging, testing, alive.

Ethan's mind raced. Military logic. PTSD logic. Rational explanation. None of it mattered here. The technology had become a conduit, the supernatural seeping into his world in ways he could see, feel, and not yet control.

He experimented cautiously, hovering his fingertips above the symbols. The circle responded, brightening where he lingered, dimming when he withdrew. The runes pulsed in time with his heartbeat. He flinched at the sensation: this was not power in the ordinary sense. It was more, a connection, a signal threading through the air, through circuits, through him.

Hours passed in tense exploration. Each time the hum surged, a drop of fear pooled in his chest. Each time the glow dimmed at his touch, a shiver of awe swept through him. Hogan lay curled at his feet, silent now, his presence grounding, though even the dog seemed alert to something in the air beyond their understanding.

By the time he leaned back in the chair, rubbing his face, sweat beading at his hairline, the cabin lights flickered, then pulsed with a low, blue-green hue. The vibration in the floor was subtle but insistent. The laptop symbol throbbed once, brighter than before, and then faded. A heartbeat. A signal. A warning.

Ethan's breath came in short, uneven bursts. He felt the weight of it all pressing down, not just the events of the past weeks, not just the eyes of the outside world, but the knowledge that something larger had chosen him, threaded through him, and would not let go.

He leaned forward, fingers brushing the pulsing circle one last time before he stepped back. The energy lingered in the air, faint and electric. Hogan's eyes tracked the glow, unblinking. Ethan's reflection shimmered in the black of the screen, the hum echoing in his chest.

Alone, he felt the magnitude of what was happening. The world outside, the technology, the ancient symbols, they were speaking, and he was listening. Or perhaps he was being called.

Either way, there was no turning back.

Ethan didn't move from the chair for a long time, eyes locked on the darkened screen. The laptop sat like a miniature altar, its pulsing symbols faintly illuminating the edges of the room. Hogan shifted beside him, ears twitching at the low-frequency hum that seemed to vibrate through the floorboards. The dog's presence, solid and warm, was the only anchor keeping Ethan from unspooling entirely.

He let his fingers hover above the laptop again, just a whisper away from contact. The moment he leaned in, the glow returned, responding to the pressure of his attention. The five-line circle, etched in light, seemed alive. It flexed, expanding slightly, then contracting like the inhale and exhale of a living thing. He felt the same tingle in his palms, the deep vibration in his chest that had accompanied the dog's revival and the boy at the lake. It was coming back, stronger, insistently.

Ethan shook his head, trying to force rationality. Computers flickered all the time. Symbols glitched. Electricity jumped. Maybe it was a virus. Maybe he was losing it. But then the soft voice, barely more than static, reached him again.

"Five... Hands..."

He leaned forward, heart hammering, hand trembling over the trackpad. The words weren't just sound, they were felt, threading into him like a needle of cold fire. Each pulse of the circle on the screen matched the rhythm of his heart. Hogan growled softly, low and warning, a sound Ethan could feel in his chest as much as hear.

Curiosity pushed him further. He reached out deliberately, fingertips brushing the laptop's surface. The glow surged instantly, and a fine vibration ran along the desk, up his arms, and pooled in his chest. His body felt weightless and heavy at the same time, as if gravity itself were bending around him. The symbols spun, faster now, and the hum in the room thickened, pushing against his eardrums.

A screen in the corner flickered to life unbidden. Images he didn't recognize flitted across it, lines of code, news feeds, social media clips. Faces of people pointing, cameras shaking, overlays of text reading

"Miracle Medic" and "Resurrection Video Goes Viral." His stomach twisted. The world had already taken notice.

Ethan's hands tingled with more than just static now, they tingled with purpose, and it terrified him. He lifted his palm slightly, experimenting. The glow responded, pulsing brighter under his fingertips, and the laptop seemed to lean toward him as if drawn. He inhaled sharply. Every instinct screamed to pull back, to flee, but he was rooted in place, mesmerized, afraid to move.

The symbols coiled, unfurling like the petals of some impossible flower, and the voice came again, sharper, clearer:

"Five... Hands... One awakens..."

Ethan's chest constricted. His rational mind scrambled for answers, military training, PTSD, any explanation, but none existed. He was touching something older than him, older than the land, older than humanity. A current of awe and terror collided in his stomach, leaving him dizzy. Hogan whined, circling his legs, and Ethan felt the dog's warmth as a tether. Without it, he might have dissolved into the floor.

He pushed further, letting the hum seep fully into his bones. It was intoxicating, and the danger of it was immediate. Each pulse of the light seemed to drain something from him, subtle but undeniable. His heart pounded in tandem with the circle, his breath coming faster. A sweat-slicked line ran down his temple. He could feel the energy spilling into him, pooling, coiling, waiting.

Then, abruptly, the circle stilled. The hum vanished. The room went dead quiet. Ethan collapsed back in the chair, fingers curling into his lap, trembling. The laptop went black, the glow extinguished as if it had never existed. Hogan nosed his shoulder, whining again, grounding him in reality.

Ethan's mind raced in a dozen directions at once. The circle. The voice. The pulse in his hands. The boy. The dog. The viral footage. Everything was converging. Everything was real.

For the first time, he let himself truly see it: the magnitude of what he had become, and the impossibility of turning away. The world outside was watching, yes, but it was also irrelevant. The force threading through him didn't care about cameras or headlines or witnesses. It cared about connection, about opening something that had been sealed for centuries.

And he was the conduit.

Hogan nudged his arm, breaking the reverie, and Ethan looked down at him. The dog's eyes were steady, almost human in their clarity. For a moment, Ethan felt small, fragile. Then, awe prickled along his spine. This life, this pulse of something beyond comprehension, was in his hands. And he had already begun to touch it.

The laptop flickered once more, faintly, a tiny ember of light in the black screen. The hum returned, just barely, a whisper beneath his ribs. He froze, staring at it, shaking, awed, terrified. The room seemed to inhale and hold its breath. And for the first time, he understood that nothing could be ordinary again.

Hogan settled by his feet, warm and solid, a grounding presence in a house that now seemed subtly, irrevocably alive. Ethan's reflection shimmered in the black screen, eyes wide, chest tight. He whispered a single word to no one in particular.

"I... don't understand."

But the hum answered anyway, faint and deliberate, like a heartbeat threading through the room. The Weave had touched him. And it was patient, waiting for the moment he could no longer ignore it.

Ethan's hands hovered over the keyboard again, even though he didn't know why. It wasn't the machine he was reaching for anymore, it was the current under the desk, the charge in the air, the subtle pressure thrumming in his bones. Every nerve ending seemed keyed to the glow that had vanished moments before, and the hum, faint but insistent, whispered under his ribs.

He touched the edge of the laptop. The screen flared violently this time, a sudden bloom of blue and gold that cast the room in stark, unnatural light. Hogan leapt back, tail tucked, ears flat, but Ethan didn't move. The light wrapped his arms, brushing across his fingers like silk and fire at once. Each pulse made the hairs on his forearms stand on end; each thrum made him feel weightless and immense at the same time.

Then the symbols appeared again. The circle, the five lines, and now runes trailing from each tip, faintly glowing like they had been carved into the very air. They weren't static; they spun, rotated, and folded in on themselves. The hum escalated, vibrating in his teeth, in his chest, in the soles of his feet. He tried to pull his hands back, and failed. The force gripped him, demanding attention, demanding acknowledgment.

The voice came through the static again, louder this time, words breaking through rational thought with jagged clarity:

"Awaken... One... The seal weakens..."

Ethan's stomach turned to ice. He realized he had no choice. The energy wasn't obeying him entirely; it was pushing, prodding, testing the boundaries. He pressed harder, fingertips digging into the desk, and suddenly a surge rocketed through him. The lights in the room flickered, the laptop shuddered, and the air smelled faintly of ozone and rain. Hogan whimpered, circling frantically.

The hum became a roar in his skull. Each breath he took, drew the glow closer to his skin. His chest burned, and for a moment he felt like he could shatter, like his body wasn't enough to contain the pulse threading through him. And then, release.

A single ripple of light leapt from the laptop to the floor, through the walls, and down the hallway, coiling like a serpent of pure energy. Pictures on the wall rattled in their frames. The fridge buzzed and clicked. His heartbeat felt shared now, synced with the pulse radiating through the house. It was as if the very walls were alive, breathing.

Ethan stumbled back, barely catching himself against the edge of the desk. Sweat poured down his face. The glow from the symbols reflected in his wide, unblinking eyes. Hogan lay low to the floor, but his tail thumped slowly, almost in rhythm with the pulsing light.

It was terrifying. And it was beautiful.

He touched the edge of the glow again, and this time it coalesced into a faint figure, human in shape but composed entirely of radiance. Its eyes were molten gold, like the woman from his dreams. Kemen. She didn't speak in words, but in meaning. Understanding rushed into him like water over a dam. The circle, the lines, the runes, they weren't just marks. They were keys. Threads connecting him to something vast and old, something that had been sleeping, waiting for touch, waiting for awareness.

Ethan's chest tightened. He tried to speak aloud, but his throat went dry. The glow pulsed again in response, drawing out the tension, weaving itself through him. He realized that every previous touch, the dog, the boy in the lake, had been small tests, minor threads of what was truly possible. He wasn't controlling it yet; he was reacting. But the reaction alone was enough to bend reality.

The symbols folded in on themselves again, folding into a single point of blinding brilliance. The hum expanded, then softened into a vibrating whisper that seemed to pulse through the floors, the walls, the air. Ethan's knees buckled. He fell to the ground, chest pressed to the floor, fingertips brushing the hum, feeling it in every fiber.

Hogan crawled close, resting his head against Ethan's shoulder. He was the only tether to the world that made sense, the only solid thing in a room alive with impossible energy. Ethan closed his eyes, letting the tremor of awe wash over him. He had been afraid, he still was, but it was awe now that grounded him, even as dread whispered that nothing would ever be ordinary again.

The laptop's screen blinked once. The glow remained, faint, almost teasing, like embers left from a fire that refused to die. Ethan could feel it lingering under his skin, in his hands, in his chest, in the pulse of the house itself. The world outside was waiting. And somehow, he knew, the Weave was waiting too, patient, inexorable, and relentless.

He whispered the words, though it felt foolish:

"Why me?"

No answer came, only the hum, only the faint pulse threading through the room, the house, the creek beyond the window. And somehow, he felt it echo back, as if the world itself were murmuring in reply.

Ethan looked down at Hogan, eyes wide, chest still heaving. The dog's ears twitched. The tail thumped once, almost in sync with the residual glow. And in that quiet, humming, post-storm moment, Ethan realized that nothing, not the viral videos, not the media, not even death itself, could touch what had begun tonight.

The Weave had touched him. And it would not let go.

12

The Weave

Ethan didn't remember falling asleep.

One moment he was sitting at the kitchen table, head in his hands, the laptop screen still flickering with static and faint geometric shapes that seemed to pulse in rhythm with his breath. The next, the chair was gone. The room was gone. The air itself had changed.

He was standing in nothing.

Not darkness, not quite. It was like standing inside the pause between lightning and thunder, a suspension of every sound and thought. Beneath his feet stretched a vast lattice of light, threads that shimmered silver and blue, crossing and knotting into a pattern so intricate his eyes couldn't follow it. Each strand hummed faintly when he moved. The vibration ran up through his legs, into his bones, a pulse that matched his heartbeat.

Far below, something moved , slow, massive, and beautiful. He looked down and saw Earth.

Clouds swirled. Oceans gleamed. The whole planet turned beneath him in silence, a living sphere wrapped in glowing filaments that connected continents, mountains, and cities in the same web that supported him. Wherever the light met, there were small, brilliant nodes, like stars burning where life was strongest.

He took a step, and the web trembled beneath him. Not fragile, responsive. As if the world itself knew he was there.

The realization hit slow and cold: *I'm dreaming.*

But it didn't feel like a dream. He felt weight. The air brushed against his skin. His pulse drummed in his throat. The smell, ozone and distant rain, was real enough to make him shiver. He crouched and touched one of the glowing threads. It was warm, pliant, vibrating softly under his fingertips. When he brushed it, sparks ran outward, tracing across the globe below, lights flaring in places he couldn't name.

Cities. Forests. Rivers.

The Weave, though he didn't know that word yet, reacted like a living nerve network. Each spark that flared below sent a faint echo back into his body. Tiny flashes of sensation; grief, laughter, pain, joy, all in a heartbeat. Too fast to separate, too human to mistake.

He jerked his hand back. The lights dimmed.

The silence that followed was absolute.

And then, far off in the endless dark above, something whispered.

Not words , not yet, just a tone, rising and falling like a breath drawn through the universe. It vibrated through the web, setting every strand trembling again. Ethan staggered to his knees, clutching his head. The sound wasn't loud; it was *inside* him, bypassing his ears completely.

When he opened his eyes, the light had changed. The web's lines glowed brighter, no longer silver, but faintly blue, the same color that had flared under his skin by the lake. The pattern spread outward, forming a circle. Five radiant lines extended from its center, crossing continents, each ending in a rune that pulsed like a heartbeat.

He recognized it instantly. It was the same sigil he'd seen on his computer screen. The same geometry that had haunted his dreams for nights.

Only now it was alive.

He stepped back instinctively, but the web beneath him shifted with him, not resisting, but *guiding*. The air felt heavy, full of expectation. Somewhere deep inside that light, he felt something watching. Not menacing, not kind, simply *aware*.

The whisper came again, this time carrying form, a voice threaded through static.

"Ethan."

He froze. The sound wasn't distant. It came from everywhere at once, woven through the very strands of light under him.

He tried to speak, to ask what this was, where he was, but his voice came out a whisper, lost in the hum. He turned slowly, scanning the vastness for any shape, any sign of life.

That was when the light began to gather.

It started at the horizon, a slow rising glow that moved like sunrise through the mesh of the Weave. It pooled and folded inward, shaping itself into a figure. The strands of light bent to her presence, aligning as if obeying gravity.

A silhouette stepped forward from the brilliance, slender, robed in shifting color, hair like liquid bronze that flowed into the air. Her eyes, when they opened, burned like the molten core of stars.

Ethan's breath caught.

Something in him, deep and old, older than his name or body, *remembered* her.

She walked toward him with the slow, measured grace of someone moving through gravity he couldn't feel. The web brightened with every step she took. Each strand beneath her feet sang.

When she spoke, her voice was both human and not, layered, as if multiple tones harmonized within it.

"The Weave endures," she said softly. "But it frays."

Ethan swallowed, his mouth dry. "Who are you?"

Her head tilted slightly, studying him. "A keeper. Once."

"Once?"

"A long time ago." Her gaze moved past him, downward to the world below. "The threads have dimmed. The world's pulse fades. You've felt it, haven't you?"

He thought of the creek's glow. The birds that moved as one. The hum that seemed to answer his heartbeat.

"I don't know what I've felt," he said.

Her expression was sorrow and relief mixed into one. "Then you still hear it. The pulse. Most have forgotten."

She raised her hand, and for a moment, the entire lattice flared with light, not painful, but breathtaking. Every intersection of the Weave shone brighter, showing places Ethan recognized faintly: rivers, mountain ranges, coastlines. Energy coursed through them like blood through veins.

"This is the Weave," she said. "The living bond of creation, every breath, every thought, every spark of life. It connects all things. You stand on what sustains your world."

Ethan shook his head, backing a step. "No. This is a dream."

Her eyes softened. "Dreams are just the places your soul remembers when you sleep."

He almost laughed, a choked sound, disbelief straining against the terror building in him. "You've got the wrong man. I'm not, whatever this is supposed to be."

"You are one of five," she said simply. "Five who bear the mark. Five whose lives touch the circle."

His stomach twisted. "I didn't ask for this."

"No one ever does."

The words hit something raw in him. The weight of every life he'd tried to save, the ones he hadn't, pressed against his chest.

He wanted to wake up. He wanted the dream gone, the world ordinary again.

But the Weave pulsed beneath his feet, steady, alive, and her eyes didn't blink.

Ethan stumbled backward on the shining lattice, breath coming ragged and shallow. The threads pulsed beneath his boots as if his heartbeat and the world's were arguing for dominance. The air trembled, vibrating with every exhale.

"I'm not..." His voice cracked. "I'm not whatever you think I am."

The vastness below answered with a slow turn of light, as if the Earth itself were listening. Every filament of the Weave responded to his voice, glowing, dimming, then surging in uneven waves. He could feel it through the soles of his feet, through his bones. It was alive, and it was listening.

Kemen stood a few paces away, her expression calm but unbearably sad. Her eyes, those impossible gold-and-emerald eyes, held something more than pity. They held knowing. "Ethan," she said softly, "you already feel it, don't you? The pulse? The way it stirs when you speak?"

"I don't feel anything." His denial came too fast. Too brittle.

Kemen tilted her head, almost tenderly. "You do."

The Weave pulsed once, hard enough to ripple the air like a bass note. Ethan staggered, grabbing at nothing. Sparks of light danced across his arms. For a heartbeat, he saw beneath the skin, tiny veins lit up like circuitry, his blood glowing faintly blue-white.

He gasped and clutched his wrist. "What is this?"

"The connection," Kemen said. "It was never gone. Just buried."

"No!" He spun on her, fury overtaking fear. "You don't get to walk into my head, my life, and tell me I'm some kind of," He couldn't finish the sentence. "I'm just a guy who lives on a farm and drinks too much coffee. I'm nobody."

Kemen's expression didn't change. "Every heartbeat in the Weave begins as one."

The words hit him like a physical blow. The threads beneath his feet flared, bleeding color into the air. The vast web surrounding him, miles, continents of light, shuddered. Lines snapped taut, then went slack, as if the world itself were holding its breath.

"You don't understand what you're asking," he said, voice breaking. "I can't, I've already failed enough people."

"You speak as if failure ends the story."

Ethan barked out a laugh that wasn't humor. "You sound just like my father."

Something in Kemen's face flickered, recognition, sorrow. "Your father's silence was not indifference. He was part of this, too. The Weave has always touched your line."

"My line?"

The light trembled again, each filament humming in answer, forming faint images that shimmered in the air: his mother's face, blurred and fading; his father's hands at a workbench; a child's toy carved from cedar, humming with faint lines of power he'd never seen before.

Ethan's throat closed. "Stop it."

"I can't," Kemen said. "It's you showing this, not me."

The images grew stronger. His childhood home flickered beneath his feet, woven from memory and starlight. He could smell the varnish, the heat of the attic, the faint ozone tang of old circuits. The Weave was pulling his life apart, thread by thread, showing him what had always been there but unseen.

"Why me?" His voice was a whisper. "Why not someone who knows what they're doing?"

"Because the world doesn't choose saints," Kemen said. "It chooses conduits."

The word rang like a bell. The entire Weave brightened, blinding, holy, terrible. Ethan dropped to his knees, hands over his head. The light poured through his fingers, through his skin, racing down the lines of his body like liquid lightning.

"Stop!"

Kemen's voice came through the roar. "You can't turn away from what's inside you. It will only find another way out."

The light erupted. The Weave convulsed, every strand firing at once. For a heartbeat, he saw it all, the whole system. Energy flowing from person to person, city to city, sky to stone to seed. The pattern stretched across time. Every connection, every life, one unbroken pulse.

And in its center, him.

Ethan screamed. Not from pain but from the enormity of it. The Weave flared in sympathy, singing like a thousand overlapping frequencies. Then, abruptly, everything dimmed.

He was left trembling on hands and knees, hair plastered to his forehead, chest heaving. The lattice under him cooled.

Kemen approached carefully, as though nearing a wounded animal. "You're afraid," she said.

"I should be."

She nodded. "Fear keeps the pulse steady. But denial breaks it."

He looked up at her, eyes raw. "And what if I break it anyway?"

Kemen smiled, a small, aching thing. "Then we all fade with you."

The Weave rippled once more, then fell silent, leaving Ethan trembling in its glow.

The silence pressed against him until he could hear only his own breath, ragged and mortal.

He closed his eyes and whispered, "I don't want this."

And somewhere, beneath his words, the Weave whispered back, soft, relentless, and alive.

The world doesn't care what you want, Ethan. Only that you listen.

The silence stretched, fragile and immense. The Weave's glow dimmed to a soft twilight shimmer, thin lines of luminescence threading through the dark like veins beneath translucent skin. Ethan stayed on his knees, staring at his hands. They trembled faintly, still threaded with the echo of light. It moved beneath the surface like trapped fireflies, pulsing with some rhythm that wasn't his own.

Kemen knelt across from him. The motion was unhurried, deliberate. The fabric of her robes brushed against the lattice, and where it touched, small ripples of light fanned outward like water disturbed. Her presence was both warmth and gravity; the closer she came, the more he felt the pull of her, an impossible mix of serenity and unbearable weight.

"Ethan," she said softly, "you can't hold the current at bay forever."

He shook his head. "It's not mine to hold."

Her eyes reflected the Weave's trembling light. "It is now."

He let out a harsh laugh that cracked in the still air. "You talk like I have a choice."

"You always did."

That quiet certainty struck deeper than any command. He turned away, looking down through the web beneath him, down at the sleeping world. Clouds drifted over continents. Cities shimmered faintly, like constellations inverted. The planet pulsed with a heartbeat he could feel through his bones.

"It's beautiful," he whispered. "And it's dying, isn't it?"

Kemen didn't answer at first. The silence was answer enough.

When she spoke, her voice trembled faintly. "Every world has its rhythm. This one is faltering. You've felt it, haven't you? In the static. The failures. The way your machines hum wrong in the dark."

Ethan's throat went dry. "That's not magic," he said. "That's entropy."

Kemen smiled faintly. "Entropy is only magic you've forgotten the name of."

The light between them brightened, thin strands connecting their shadows. He saw the faint outline of the circle again, the same one that had burned across his computer screen, the five lines radiating outward like the spokes of an unseen sun. It hovered in the air now, ghostly and alive.

Kemen lifted her hand. Her fingers shimmered, translucent at the edges, as though she were made of the same luminous material as the Weave itself.

Ethan flinched back instinctively. "Don't."

But she didn't lower her hand. "You fear what's already within you. Let me show you it can be borne."

He tried to speak, but the words tangled in his throat. There was nowhere to run, no direction in this impossible sky that wasn't already wrapped in light. The Weave pulsed once, slowly, like a breath.

Her hand reached his chest.

Contact.

The world went silent.

The sensation wasn't heat or pressure but something deeper, like the moment between heartbeats when time forgets to move. Her palm rested over his sternum, and for a second he thought he felt nothing at all. Then it began, a deep, resonant vibration that spread outward through his ribs, his lungs, his spine.

The Weave responded in kind. Every strand in sight flared white. Lines shot outward, converging on the point where her hand met his chest. The symbol bloomed there, five lines radiating from a single circle, drawn in light, alive and shifting.

Ethan gasped. The vibration became a burn, intense, electric, pure. His vision fractured. He saw layers of himself, skin, muscle, spirit, each glowing with filaments that spiraled outward to join the Weave. He wasn't separate anymore. The boundary between self and system dissolved like fog under sun.

He tried to push her away, but his hand met resistance like glass. She held him there, eyes locked on his, unblinking. "Breathe," she said.

"I, can't... "

"Breathe."

The command wasn't forceful. It was inevitable. His lungs obeyed. Air flowed in, and with it came something vast, something ancient and endless. The Weave inhaled with him.

He saw faces, countless and fleeting, human and not. He saw the pulse of stars collapsing into the rhythm of rain. He saw code and prayer as the same language. He saw that every thought, every act of love or cruelty, every whisper carried through the fabric of existence, left a mark in the same current now burning through his chest.

He screamed. Not from pain, but from knowing.

The rune on his chest flared like molten gold. The Weave shrieked, a soundless thunder rolling through eternity, and then everything shattered into silence.

When he opened his eyes again, Kemen's hand was still there, resting lightly against his skin. The symbol was still glowing, though dimmer now, seared into him like a brand of light.

"It will fade," she murmured, "but never vanish. It will answer when you call, and sometimes when you don't."

He stared at her, dazed. "What did you do to me?"

"I didn't give you anything new," she said. "I only uncovered what you buried."

The air smelled of ozone and rain. The Weave around them dimmed, its glow softening to a muted pulse, like the slowing of a vast heartbeat.

Ethan looked down at his chest. The rune's glow pulsed faintly, matching his breath. He could feel it in his veins, like a whisper threading through his blood. It wasn't pain now. It was presence.

Kemen leaned closer, her voice barely audible. "You are not the savior, Ethan. You are the bridge."

He wanted to ask what that meant, but words failed him. She was already fading, her form dissolving into motes of light, each one drifting upward into the luminous lattice.

"Kemen,"

"Listen," she said, her voice a fading echo. "The world is calling. You only have to answer."

Then she was gone.

The Weave trembled once more, a sigh through eternity, and then it all collapsed into darkness.

The fall was silent.

The last thing he felt before everything dissolved was the slow, steady pulse beneath his skin, his heartbeat and the world's, fused into one.

The scream tore him out of the void.

Ethan shot upright in bed, drenched in sweat, the sound still echoing in his throat. For a heartbeat he didn't recognize the room, the pale shapes of the walls, the thin dawn light leaking through the curtains, the slow tick of the clock on the nightstand. His lungs stuttered, pulling air that felt too heavy, too bright.

Hogan was barking at the foot of the bed, hackles up, teeth bared toward the empty air. The room smelled faintly of ozone and damp earth, as if a thunderstorm had just passed through the house.

Ethan clutched his chest.

It was hot beneath his palm, skin searing with a low, steady burn. He pulled his hand back and stared. There, faint but unmistakable, glowed the symbol: a circle with five lines radiating outward, etched in light beneath the skin like bioluminescent scar tissue.

"No..." His voice cracked. "No, no, no..."

He stumbled from the bed, nearly tripping over Hogan as he crossed to the mirror. The dog whined, pacing, still growling low in his throat. Ethan leaned close to the glass, the pale morning reflection trembling with every ragged breath.

The mark pulsed. Once. Twice. Then settled into rhythm, his rhythm.

Every beat of his heart sent a faint shimmer of light through the pattern, like phosphorescence rippling across water. For an instant, he thought he could *hear* it, a low hum under the edge of silence, the same tone he'd heard in the dream. The Weave breathing through him.

He gripped the counter to steady himself. His reflection wavered, blurred, then briefly doubled, two Ethans staring back: one human and exhausted, the other faintly luminescent, eyes threaded with light. The image flickered, then collapsed back to one.

The sound in the room changed. The clock stuttered. The bulb in the lamp above the sink flared and dimmed in time with his pulse. From the kitchen, the refrigerator compressor kicked on, then stopped dead, humming a single sustained note that shouldn't have been possible.

Hogan barked again, backing toward the hallway.

"Easy, boy," Ethan rasped, though his voice carried no conviction.

He turned on the faucet. The water came out in fits, spurts, then a shimmer of something like silver in the stream. He blinked hard, and it was gone.

The mark pulsed again.

And beneath it, just for an instant, he felt *her hand.* The memory of it. The warmth. The weight.

He doubled over, gripping the sink, chest heaving.

"It wasn't real," he whispered. "It was a dream. Just a dream..."

But even as he said it, the air around him seemed to bend. The hum deepened, vibrating through the glass, through the pipes, through the *walls.* His phone buzzed on the nightstand, screen lighting up with notifications, one after another.

He stumbled back into the bedroom and grabbed it.

The lock screen flashed with dozens of missed messages, news alerts, social feeds, and emails. One stood out, timestamped just minutes ago:

"Miracle Medic Rescuer Caught in Strange Light Phenomenon."

A still frame accompanied the headline: the security camera from the hospital's rear lot. In the grainy image, Ethan stood by his truck, hand to his chest. A faint, bluish glow radiated outward, lighting the pavement and the surrounding trees.

It wasn't just a dream. It had followed him back.

Ethan sank to the floor. Hogan pressed against his side, trembling. The house was utterly still, save for that hum, the sound under everything, low and omnipresent, threading through the wires, through the air itself.

He lifted his hand again, staring at the faint light beneath his skin.

It pulsed once more, matching the rhythm of his heart.

And somewhere, distant yet immediate, like a whisper carried on wind, he heard Kemen's voice.

"The world is calling. You only have to answer."

The light flared, brighter, then gone.

The hum ceased. The house returned to silence.

Ethan sat in the dim light of morning, shaking, his breath fogging the air. Outside, the first birds had begun to sing again, but they sounded wrong, off-key, like a choir trying to remember a forgotten tune.

He stared down at the faintly glowing symbol over his heart.

The Weave wasn't a dream. It was awake.

And now, so was he.

13

Fractures

Ethan's hands gripped the worn steering wheel, knuckles pale beneath the callouses. The Tennessee backroads stretched ahead like ribbons of gray silk through the pine shadows, interrupted only by the occasional white line fading under cracked asphalt. The night was cool, the air carrying the tang of rain that had fallen hours earlier. He drove not toward anywhere in particular, only away from the oppressive quiet of his cabin.

Every mile, his thoughts circled the same pattern: Hogan, the boy in the lake, the glowing runes, the whispering woman in his dreams. He tried to shake them off, telling himself it was adrenaline, hallucination, whatever rational explanation could survive after the viral footage. But the hum under his skin, the pulse in his fingers, he could no longer lie to himself. Something inside him had changed, and that something wasn't human.

The headlights caught movement before he even registered it, a blur of black and silver across the lane. Reflex took over.

The car swerved, tires screaming against asphalt. Ethan didn't think; he acted. The sound of impact was muted but suffocating, a dull thump in the chest as his body followed instinct. Glass shattered, the smell of burned rubber and wet earth mixing with blood and oil.

He climbed out, heartbeat hammering, and saw them: two vehicles twisted against each other, their metal bent like paper. Smoke rose from the crumpled hood of a pickup. Ethan's eyes fell on the victims before his mind could catch up.

One man was pinned, face pale, chest rising in shallow, ragged gasps. A woman slumped against the steering wheel of a compact car, unmoving. He didn't pause. His hands went out almost before he could think.

The familiar hum surged in his veins, radiating from fingertips to every nerve ending. He pressed his palms to the man's chest. Heat flowed, a river of power he hadn't fully measured, of life itself threading through him. The man's eyes fluttered and then opened. Breath returned in shaky gulps, a return from the edge.

Ethan pulled back, sweat slicking his forehead, adrenaline spiking against the strange, growing terror inside. But the woman remained unmoved, her chest still. He felt it before his eyes confirmed it: the life was leaving her, siphoned away by the same invisible current that had revived the man. His stomach turned; nausea clawed.

"No, no, no," he whispered, stumbling backward. He had healed and killed in the same instant, and the realization sank into his bones.

Ethan collapsed to the gravel shoulder, fingers digging into the dirt. The sensation was visceral, a sharp, jagged pain that radiated from his chest outward, as if the world itself had split open inside him. He could feel it: the man breathing, the woman gone, the energy he'd poured into life only to have death follow in tandem.

Hogan appeared, barking once, running to him and circling his legs, eyes wide and alert. Ethan barely registered the dog; he was consumed by the shuddering rhythm of life and death alternating through him.

A scream tore from his throat, half panic, half raw disbelief. His body convulsed, the aftershocks of power wracking him. He vomited, bitter blood and bile spilling onto his hands. The taste burned, metallic and impossible, and he recoiled.

The scene around him blurred. Streetlights flickered in rhythm with the pulse in his chest, the surreal vibration that had followed him since Hogan, since the boy in the lake, now a living, unbearable cadence. He tried to lift himself to his feet, legs weak, knees scraped.

The highway was quiet again. Too quiet. Emergency sirens approached, but he knew they were not for him. They were for the survivors, for the living world that had continued without regard for the subtle, terrible force inside him.

Ethan's hands shook as he touched his chest. A faint glow lingered, the echo of the rune, a whisper of the Weave still present in his veins. He shivered, not from cold, but from awe and dread interwoven. He had crossed a line; there was no going back.

The hum under his skin pulsed in response to the world around him. Each heartbeat was a tiny fracture in his understanding, in his soul. He could heal. He could kill. And he would feel both, forever.

Hogan nudged his hand, a warm, living weight. Ethan looked down at the dog, eyes wide. Fear, disbelief, and awe tangled in the silent night. The Weave was real. It had chosen him, or perhaps it had just awakened, and he was merely the conduit.

He stared at Hogan, trembling, and whispered, barely audibly, "What... what have I become?"

The night held its breath. Somewhere down the road, lights flickered. A pulse, a shimmer, almost imperceptible, ran along the asphalt. Ethan felt it in his chest. The Weave had left a mark. And it was waiting.

14

The Network

The hum of fluorescent lights in the DHS operations center was sharp in Ethan's ears, though he wasn't here. Not physically, anyway. In the backroads of Tennessee, miles from any city, he pressed the heel of his hand to his temple, feeling the thrum of energy he didn't understand pulse faintly beneath his skin. A hum in his skull that never seemed to stop.

Inside the government building, monitors flickered, each replaying the same footage from different angles: the lake, the highway crash, the tiny miracle at the vet's office. Analysts sat shoulder to shoulder, faces tight with disbelief.

"This is... unprecedented," one muttered, fingers hovering over the keyboard. Infrared layers over the lake footage showed his pulse faintly visible, a shimmer across the boy's chest. "Whoever this guy is, he's... not human."

Another analyst shook his head. "Not human, maybe. Not a terrorist. He's scared. Look at the footage. Look at him."

Ethan's hands, when they touched the steering wheel of his old pickup, tensed and tingled. He didn't know why. His nerves were keyed to something deeper than fear now, a resonance that mirrored the hum of machines miles away, in offices he'd never see. Somewhere, the circle with five lines, the rune, throbbed in his memory like a pulse he couldn't quite reach.

The analysts typed furiously, tagging, cross-referencing, overlaying city maps and traffic reports. Every anomalous event in the past twenty-four hours led back to him.

"DHS," the team leader muttered, staring at the screen with hard eyes. "He's a national security anomaly. Bring him in... alive. No mistakes."

Cole Ramirez leaned back in his chair, rubbing the crease between his eyes. He read the briefing, scrolled through the incident files, and watched the clips again. Lake rescue. Highway crash. Dog revival. Plants flowering in seconds. And yet, it wasn't fear he felt. Empathy.

"This guy," he muttered, more to himself than the empty room, "he's scared. He's not a terrorist. He doesn't even know what he is."

He tapped the screen. Infrared shots of Ethan's hands pulsing faintly blue. Motion-tracking overlays showing energy radiating outward, dissipating over yards. Ramirez's stomach knotted. This was beyond anything in the manual. Biological anomaly. Potentially weaponizable. Dangerous. But the fear he saw in Ethan's eyes, he recognized that. He'd seen it before, back in field ops, when young men faced things bigger than themselves and had no choice but to act.

"Bring him in alive," the order repeated itself in his mind. "Alive." But Ramirez didn't feel the same resolve the brass felt. There was something human at stake here. Something more than control.

By mid-afternoon, Ethan had returned to his cabin. The sky was muted gray, clouds heavy and low. The wind tugged at the trees like fingers through cloth. He could feel the world listening now, every leaf, every shadow keyed into the same hum pulsing through his hands.

He packed: a backpack of essentials, Hogan at his heels, pacing, ears flicking to the invisible. Ethan's heart hammered with a primitive, urgent rhythm, survival instinct, honed in Afghanistan, but now tinged with something else.

The power flickered. A lamp jumped, the filament glowing blue for a heartbeat, then normal. Papers on the table shifted slightly, as if an unseen draft had brushed past. Ethan froze.

"No," he muttered. "No, I'm not crazy."

But the humming didn't stop. Every heartbeat brought it closer. Every breath made it louder. His fingers brushed the zipper of his backpack and the leather strap seemed to pull itself taut, vibrating faintly. Hogan whined, circling closer.

Ethan glanced around the cabin. The walls seemed too close now, the air too thick. Every shadow moved just a little against his peripheral vision. Small objects lifted, hovered, then fell. His chest tightened.

He swallowed. He had to leave. But even as he stepped outside, he knew the world had already moved against him, mapped him, felt him.

By the time he reached the ridge above the creek, the exhaustion hit. The tension of the past hours, the rush of energy through his fingers, the constant hum of anticipation, all came together like a weight pressing on his skull.

He sank to the ground. Hogan nudged him once, then sat silently, watching. And then, he passed out.

In the darkness behind his eyelids, the world unfolded like a web of light. Strings, filaments, glowing threads connected every city, every human pulse, every living thing. And somewhere in the vastness, he was the center. His heartbeat resonated through the network, felt everywhere.

The threads snapped in places. Cities flickered into shadow. People froze mid-motion, whispers of life disappearing into nothingness. He wanted to scream but couldn't. The scale of it was impossible.

And then, a voice. Distant, echoing, resonant: *"Five Hands. One of five. You are its nexus."*

Ethan's stomach clenched. He recognized the hum, the vibration in his hands, the pull he'd felt all day. It was part of this. He was part of this.

He woke hours later, sprawled on the ridge, Hogan licking his face. The wind had changed. The creek was calm again, but the air thrummed with residual energy. The world seemed ordinary on the surface, but Ethan knew differently now. He could feel it, everything was connected, fragile, and he was at the heart of it.

His hands still tingled. And the hum... the hum never left.

Ethan rose slowly, chest tight, eyes scanning the horizon. Hogan sat obediently beside him, tail still, ears up. The first lights of evening flickered across the creek, bending in an impossible way, shadows dancing as if alive.

He ran a finger across the top of a fallen leaf. It shimmered faintly, an echo of the Weave's pulse. Ethan shivered, awe and dread coiling in equal measure.

Somewhere beyond the trees, beyond the roads, the world waited. And it was watching him.

The hum under Ethan's skin never stopped. Even as he stumbled along the creek bank, each footstep heavy with adrenaline and dread, he felt it vibrating through him like a wire strung taut. Hogan padded beside him, ears alert, tail low but stiff. The dog's presence was grounding, a reminder of something living and ordinary in a world that no longer made sense.

Across the state, in the DHS command center, monitors displayed overlays of heat signatures, IR scans, and video footage. Ramirez leaned over the main console, fingers tracing Ethan's path on a map. Each anomaly was a spike, a flare of impossible energy. Each spike led back to him.

"We're not dealing with a normal suspect," one tech whispered, eyes wide behind her glasses. "We're... tracking a living phenomenon."

Ramirez felt the same knot in his stomach he always did when tasked with impossible jobs. Not fear, exactly. Respect for the unknown, maybe, or empathy for the frightened human at the center of it. "He's not a threat yet," Ramirez said, more to himself than anyone else. "He's scared. That's all."

Back on the dirt road, Ethan's fingers grazed the hood of his truck. It vibrated faintly beneath his touch. The world around him seemed alive, bending slightly, flickering in ways that made him blink. Hogan whined softly, brushing against his leg, his brown eyes wide, reflecting the filtered light of a low sun.

Ethan took a shaky breath. *He's watching. Something is always watching.*

A branch snapped. Hogan leapt, teeth bared, tail straight. Ethan's pulse spiked. A deer bolted from the brush, its hooves striking the dirt with a rhythm that matched the thrum in his skull. Every bird call, every rustle in the leaves, amplified the humming energy in his palms. He could feel it now: not just in his hands, but coursing through his entire nervous system, like electricity dancing over his skin.

The backpack was heavy, full of water, a few cans, and clothes. But it felt like lead in his arms. His head spun, vision blurring. Hogan stayed close, nuzzling him, grounding him to the reality he could still touch. The creek beside them shimmered faintly, the surface glinting as if the light itself were fractured.

Ethan's attention was caught by the distant wail of sirens. Heart hammering, he ducked behind a stand of trees. Across the highway, a crash had already happened. Smoke rose in lazy spirals, punctuated by the staccato of car alarms. Ethan froze. He knew what to do before he even thought it.

The hum surged, rising in pitch, radiating from his chest to his hands. His fingers tingled, the air around them shimmering. Hogan growled low in his throat. Ethan stepped forward.

People were trapped. Glass sparkled like shards of ice. One man was pinned beneath a twisted doorframe. Ethan's hands hovered over him instinctively. The hum thrummed faster, a heartbeat that matched his own.

Energy surged through him. Pain, warmth, heat, something unnameable. The man gasped, air flooding his lungs. Ethan felt a tug, a pull toward life itself, but it came with cost. A second man, farther down the highway, stopped moving. His body slackened, chest still. Ethan felt it, a drain through his nervous system. The Weave exacted its price.

Hogan stayed at his side, barking, unsettled. Ethan's stomach twisted. He pressed the heels of his hands into his temples. He could feel both lives, one revived, one slipping away. The sensation was dizzying, nauseating, terrifying.

He stumbled back into the dirt. Hogan licked his face, a comforting constant against the chaos. Ethan breathed in the smoke and burnt rubber, trying to steady the tremors running through him. He wanted to run, hide, vanish, but he also knew, he could never undo what he had done.

In the DHS operations center, Ramirez leaned closer to the screens. Every camera across the state that had caught flashes of light or strange anomalies now tracked the energy trail left by Ethan's hands. Security footage from nearby stores captured faint, pulsing auras surrounding him. It was as if reality itself bent toward him, acknowledging the presence of something inhuman.

"He's a conduit," one tech said, awe mixed with fear. "Everything near him responds. Plants. Electronics. Weather anomalies. We can't approach him safely."

Ramirez rubbed his eyes, thinking back to the boy in the lake, the dog, the crash. Fear wasn't part of it anymore; respect and dread had replaced it. And yet, he knew orders were orders. Ethan had to be contained. Alive, if possible.

Back on the road, Ethan's vision blurred as the pulse intensified. The hum became a roar, a resonance with the creek, the trees, the very earth. Hogan whined, pacing circles around him, tail stiff. Ethan pressed both hands to the ground. The energy flowed beneath his palms, into the soil, over the rocks, connecting everything.

It's all connected.

The world tilted, and Ethan's knees buckled. Hogan barked sharply, nipping at his jacket, trying to pull him upright. But he collapsed anyway, unconscious before he hit the dirt.

In the blackness behind his eyelids, the world unfolded. Massive threads of glowing light stretched across continents, cities, rivers, forests, the Earth itself pulsed with them. And at the center, a point of light, faint but insistent, corresponded to him.

He was the heartbeat.

Filaments snapped in places, lights fading, humans frozen midstep, trees tilting unnaturally. The weight of it was suffocating. Ethan wanted to scream, but no sound emerged.

And then, a voice, echoing across the threads, resonant and familiar:

"Five Hands. One of five. You are its nexus."

The hum inside him became unbearable, then collapsed into a single, overwhelming beat. He felt the energy, the responsibility, the impossibility of it.

Ethan woke hours later, sprawled on the ridge above his creek, Hogan nudging his face, tail wagging faintly. The air smelled of wet earth, the creek lapping quietly in the distance. But the hum never left. Every heartbeat echoed it.

He rose slowly, hands trembling, feeling the residual pull of the Weave. Small branches twitched, leaves shimmered faintly as if vibrating with the invisible network he now knew existed. The world seemed calm, ordinary even, but he knew better.

Hogan sat beside him, unwavering, alert. Ethan's fingers brushed the dirt, and for a brief instant, the soil glimmered faintly, a pulse echoing the rhythm inside him.

He swallowed hard. The hum in his veins was a promise, a warning, a call. He was the nexus. And the network was alive. Watching. Waiting.

Ethan turned his gaze across the creek, the ridge, the distant road, feeling awe, dread, and responsibility coil together like fire in his chest. Hogan rested at his feet, breathing calm, tethering him to the human world. Yet Ethan understood, the Weave had chosen him. There was no escape.

And somewhere, faintly, across miles of reality, the pulse of the network answered.

15

Lila's Choice

Ethan was slumped against the doorframe of his truck, the metal biting cold against his back. Hogan circled him once, then sat on his haunches, ears pricked, tail flicking nervously. The world was quiet except for the occasional creak of the old wooden barn doors in the distance, the restless wind in the trees, and the soft thrum of something deeper, the faint pulse in the air he hadn't been able to control since the lake.

Lila's truck rolled to a stop behind his, tires crunching over gravel. She jumped out before the engine had even cooled, boots thumping on the dirt. "Ethan!" Her voice was sharp with concern but steady, the calm he hadn't realized he was craving.

He lifted his head just enough to see her, felt the weight in his chest tighten. She knelt without a word, hands steady as she brushed a strand of hair from his forehead. "Let's get you back inside."

Hogan nudged his hand, whining softly. Ethan didn't respond, not at first. His hands shook too violently to obey. Lila's presence was an anchor, but one he couldn't quite trust. One wrong movement, and whatever lingering pulse he carried could, he didn't know. Could destroy.

Inside the cabin, the air smelled faintly of old wood and creek water. Lila helped him to a chair, sank beside him, and pulled a damp cloth over his forehead. "You're burning out," she said softly. No judgment, no accusation. Just statement.

Ethan's eyes, still hazy, caught her face, the familiar curve of her mouth, the steady brown eyes that had examined Hogan hours ago without blinking. "I..." His voice cracked. He shook his head. "I don't know what's happening to me."

"You're human," she said, almost too quietly. "But I've seen things... I believe there's more to this. What you did for that dog, for that boy..." She hesitated, glancing down at Hogan, then back at him. "I've never seen anything like it."

Ethan exhaled slowly, the weight in his chest tightening further. "I'm... I'm scared, Lila. Every time it happens, I feel it pull something out of me, like I'm bleeding life into someone else." His hand twitched; Hogan leaned into him instinctively.

"You're not alone," she said, placing her hand over his. The warmth was sharp and immediate. "Not in this. But you can't keep going without rest. You'll kill yourself before you even understand what this is."

He tried to meet her gaze, but fear was knotting inside him. She believed, she trusted, but she didn't understand the cost. "You have no idea. God wouldn't pick someone like me. Not someone who..." He trailed off, shaking his head. The images of the boy, the dog, the crash, he couldn't unsee them.

Lila leaned closer, her presence steadying the tremor in his chest. "I don't know how it works, Ethan. But I see you. And I believe in what you can do."

It was enough to make his chest ache. Human connection. Something he hadn't allowed himself in years. He closed his eyes, letting her presence soak into him.

The words came out almost involuntarily. "I saw... a woman. She said 'One of Five. The seal thins.'" His voice was hoarse, tremulous. "I don't know what it means. I don't even know if I want to know."

Lila's hand stayed on his. "Maybe you're not supposed to understand yet. Maybe you just have to... survive."

He looked up at her, at the worry etched across her face, and something fragile, fleeting, opened in him. But he pulled back. Always the pullback. "You can't get close to a live wire," he said, voice low, almost a whisper.

She didn't flinch. Instead, she brushed her fingers against his cheek. "Then I'll just stand here and keep the ground steady for when it burns out."

Hogan moved between them, curling at Ethan's feet, nose pressed against his boot. The faint hum in the room tickled at the edges of his awareness, a tremor in the air he couldn't ignore. Lights flickered once, briefly, casting long shadows against the walls. He flinched, but Lila didn't. She just tightened her hand on his.

The creek outside hissed softly in the dark, the water reflecting moonlight like it was aware of something beneath its surface. Ethan felt the pull again, the energy coiling in his chest, not enough to touch yet, but enough to remind him of the cost. Every heartbeat was a warning, every pulse a threat.

He swallowed hard, voice barely audible. "If it grows... I can't promise you'll be safe."

"I know," she said simply. "But I'll take the risk. I believe in you."

For a long moment, he allowed himself to imagine what that meant: human trust, faith without certainty, a tether to something real in a world that was fracturing at the edges. But the hum persisted, the faint shimmer in the air around him, and he remembered, he could heal, but every act cost him, sometimes more than he could bear.

He exhaled, closing his eyes as Hogan leaned closer, his body warm against Ethan's legs. The room was quiet except for the creek's distant rush, the faint hum of the Weave threading around him, and the steady, reassuring presence of Lila.

He opened his eyes again, staring at the glow in the air, the pulse under his skin, the dog at his feet, and the woman he trusted sitting across from him. Awe, dread, and fragile hope collided. For the first time in a long while, he allowed himself to sit in the paradox, that he could be human, and something more, all at once.

The lights flickered once more, softly, like a heartbeat. Hogan's ears twitched; Lila's eyes held his. Ethan shivered. He was still terrified, still aware of the danger that lingered in him. But for this moment, he was not entirely alone.

And that was enough.

16

Shadows of War

The creek ran sluggish and dark under the rain, winding its way past the edge of Ethan's property like a vein of water through bruised earth. He walked along the bank, boots sinking into the wet soil, each step heavier than the last. The night pressed close, damp and cold, carrying a low hum that seemed to vibrate in his chest, not just in the air. He didn't know if it was the storm, the energy that had been following him, or the echo of something deeper, something inside himself he had never truly faced.

Hogan walked silently at his side, fur slick with rain, eyes bright and attentive. Ethan barely noticed. His mind churned with fragments of the day: the boy in the lake, the viral footage, the weight of the invisible world pressing against him. He wanted to run, to hide, to leave it all behind, but he couldn't. Wherever the energy went, it followed. Wherever he went, it whispered.

And then he saw them.

At first, they were just shadows. Tall, solid figures that flitted between the trees, glimpses of movement that made him blink twice, thinking the storm was playing tricks. Then the shapes solidified, faces, uniforms, guns slung across shoulders. Familiar shapes. Familiar faces.

His stomach clenched.

Ethan froze. They weren't alive. They couldn't be. And yet there they were, marching in silence, lining the creek as though standing guard. Their eyes, when they met his, were filled with accusation and sorrow, heavy with unspoken words.

"You couldn't save us then..." one seemed to say, the phrase vibrating in the back of his skull rather than through sound. "...Why now?"

Ethan's hands clenched at his sides. His pulse jumped. The hum in the air rose, responding to the knot of guilt in his chest. He tried to tell himself it was memory, PTSD kicking back hard after the viral videos and the unrelenting strain of his power, but it felt too vivid, too sharp. The air itself seemed alive, shimmering faintly along the edges of the rain.

He took a step forward, and the reflections in the creek rippled unnaturally, as if the water itself acknowledged the presence of the dead. Hogan growled softly, ears flat, tail tucked, circling him in a protective arc. The dog had seen enough to know something was wrong, had felt enough energy to sense that this was more than hallucination.

Ethan's throat tightened. "I, " he swallowed, but no sound came. His mind spun back to Afghanistan, to the rivers under fire, the screaming, the orders shouted over machine-gun bursts. He had been a medic then, hands trembling, heart hammering, powerless to save everyone. Every body lost, every friend ripped from him, pressed into his chest like stones.

And now the energy within him pulsed, matching that same rhythm, life and death tied to him, flowing through his body, waiting for his command, waiting for him to falter.

"You couldn't save us then... why now?" The phrase echoed again, louder this time, punctuated by the beat of rain on leaves, on the creek.

Ethan staggered backward. The energy around him flared involuntarily. Leaves shivered, water glowed faintly, and lightning arced across the sky like a finger pointing at him. His vision blurred, and the faces of the ghosts, of the men he had failed, seared themselves into his mind.

He tried to run, tried to focus on the ground beneath his boots, but each step seemed heavier than the last. The hum in the air grew insistent, vibrating along the wet metal of his truck, vibrating through Hogan's fur and into his own chest. It was a chorus of everything he had suppressed, fear, guilt, and sorrow intertwined with the residue of the Weave itself.

He fell to his knees at the edge of the creek, water soaking through his pants. Hands pressed into mud; he tasted the iron tang of soil and blood. And then, as if it had been waiting, the energy surged fully. His hands glowed faintly in the dark, rippling with that impossible heat, warm yet terrible. Hogan whined and pressed against him, nose nudging at his wrist, but even the dog seemed cautious now, aware of the force coursing through its master.

Ethan buried his face in his hands. The tears came freely, mixing with the rain. He felt the pulse of the dead soldiers, the pulse of his own guilt, and the pull of something vast and living through the Weave. His stomach churned, nausea blooming with the growing hum. He vomited into the creek, the cold water washing over him, taste of iron sharp on his tongue.

"I can't," he whispered through ragged breaths, "I can't do this."

The wind tore through the trees, shaking branches and rattling the rain against the roof of the distant barn. The spectral soldiers pressed closer in his mind, silent but accusing. And then, a movement at the periphery: a figure in the rain, lit by a flash of lightning. Lila.

She ran through the wet field, hands outstretched. "Ethan!" Her voice cut through the storm, real and solid, grounding him more than he realized he needed. Hogan bounded ahead, circling her legs, barking, and then leaping back to Ethan's side. The presence of another human being, living and breathing, stabilized the torrent of energy swirling around him.

He collapsed fully into her arms, drenched, shaking, and finally allowed himself to let go. He felt her warmth, her steady heartbeat, the rhythm of her breathing, and for the first time in hours, his own pulse slowed slightly. The glow in his hands dimmed to a faint flicker, the hum softened, though it lingered, a reminder of the force that would not be ignored.

"I..." Ethan choked, voice rough. "I can't control it. I don't know how."

"You're human," Lila said softly, pressing a hand to his chest, over the faintly glowing rune that had begun to appear there weeks ago. "Even if it feels like you're not, you are. You're alive. You're here."

He shivered against her, letting the rain soak him, letting the tears fall. Hogan nuzzled his neck, whining softly, a tether to the tangible world. The ghosts of the past lingered at the edges of his vision, distant and insistent, but their grip had loosened, held at bay by the warmth of another living heart.

Ethan's eyes swept across the creek. The water shimmered faintly, as if acknowledging the storm of energy that had passed through him. Trees trembled, mud slid under his hands, and the rain fell in silver threads. He was exhausted, terrified, and yet... awed. The Weave pulsed in quiet, subtle acknowledgment, a hum just below perception, echoing across the creek and through him.

"I, " he began, but words failed him. Only the low vibration of the air and the soft breathing of the two beings who had anchored him remained.

Lila tightened her hold, and for the first time, he allowed himself to accept the possibility: that even amidst the guilt, the haunting memories, and the raw, uncontrollable power inside him, he was not completely alone.

Hogan shifted, curling against his legs, ears twitching as the last of the spectral whispering ebbed into the wind. The energy in the air pulsed once more, faint and rhythmic, like a heartbeat mirrored in the creek. Ethan looked at it, wide-eyed, a mixture of dread and awe pulling tight in his chest.

And then the storm eased.

The night was still, save for the soft rush of water over rocks and the distant rattle of leaves. Rain dripped from his hair and soaked into the soil beneath him, but the oppressive hum had lessened, leaving a residue that vibrated faintly through his skin. It was a whisper now, the echo of the Weave, and for the first time he felt the weight of it, not just as power, but as responsibility.

He pressed a hand against the wet earth, feeling Hogan's fur, Lila's warmth, and the faint pulse beneath his chest. The ghosts were gone, but their presence lingered, as did the reminder that he could never go back to being just a man.

The creek shimmered faintly, reflecting a sky bruised by storm clouds and moonlight. Ethan's hands glowed once, briefly, a ripple of light that faded into nothing. And he understood, with an awe that was both exhilarating and terrifying: the Weave was awake, and he was part of it.

Hogan whined softly and nuzzled his hand. Lila's gaze met his, unflinching, steady. And for a long moment, Ethan let himself breathe, drenched and trembling, caught between dread and wonder.

The shadows of war had passed through him tonight. But the hum remained.

And it would not be silent for long.

17

Conduit

The morning sunlight slid through the thin curtains of Ethan's cabin, touching the floor in streaks of amber. The creek behind the house murmured faintly, a quiet undercurrent to the soft stirring of the world. He lay on the cot, breathing shallow, counting the rise and fall of his chest like it was the only tether to sanity. Hogan lay curled at his feet, tail twitching, ears pricked. The dog had been with him since the lake, since the first undeniable spark of life had flowed through him.

The quiet felt heavy, not peaceful. Ethan could still feel the echoes of the crash, the boy's wet hair, the pulse in his palms. He flexed his fingers and there it was again, a faint hum, as if the world itself was vibrating beneath the skin. It wasn't pain, exactly, but the sense of a current moving through his body, an invisible tide he couldn't fully command.

Hogan shifted, sniffing the air near Ethan's hands. The dog's attention was unwavering, alert to things Ethan couldn't yet name. For a brief second, the cabin felt like a vessel, Hogan its sentinel, Ethan both passenger and conduit. He sat up, pressing a palm to his chest. The hum deepened, a low, resonant thrum that made the floorboards seem alive beneath him.

He whispered, almost without thinking: "It's still there."

By mid-morning, Ethan was in the small clearing by the cabin, a bundle of energy coiled tight in his chest. The creek reflected the sun in broken glimmers, and the gentle hum in the air made the hairs on his arms stand on end. He knelt beside a fern, dry and brittle from the lingering cold of spring nights and laid a hand over it.

Nothing happened at first. He pulled back, heart hammering. "You're imagining it," he muttered. But the leaves twitched again, curling slightly before straightening. The green deepened, the fern almost imperceptibly vibrant.

Hogan whined softly, circling Ethan's legs, then pressed his nose to the fern. His tail wagged once, tentative, cautious.

Ethan exhaled shakily. The sensation in his chest surged, a warm pulse spreading outward, as if his own life force was threading into the plant. He could feel it, the tiny energy spike, the faint thrill of creation. The hum followed him like a tide, vibrating in the air, in his bones.

"Okay," he whispered. "Okay."

He reached for a fallen bird feather nearby, small and brittle. His fingers brushed it, and the barbs shimmered faintly, lifting into the air for a heartbeat, then settling again. Hogan barked softly, the sound punctuating the strange quiet, the dog's ears forward, eyes wide.

Ethan's hands trembled. He had no manual, no guide. Nothing to explain what should have been impossible, yet here it was. Every breath drew in awe and panic together, in equal measure.

By noon, Ethan had moved inside, pacing the cabin with Hogan at his heels. Each attempt to coax life from something small left him drained, dizzy, nauseous, as though each pulse of power siphoned from his own body. A dying fern, a fallen beetle, he tried to nudge both, and felt the faint recoil of vitality leave him.

His chest burned faintly, heart racing, the world tilting slightly on its axis. He staggered to the counter, bracing his hands, closing his eyes. Hogan leaned against him, steadying presence, fur warm against his side.

The thought struck him then, sudden and undeniable: *Every act costs me something.*

He swallowed hard. The idea should have paralyzed him, and for a moment it almost did. But instead, a sharp clarity pierced the haze of fear. This power, the flow through him, was real. Terrible, exquisite, overwhelming.

The cabin vibrated subtly, the air thickened with a faint hum, like electricity in a storm. Hogan's ears twitched; the dog sniffed at the air, nostrils flaring. The energy around Ethan was no longer subtle. It pulsed faintly, reacting to his mood, his thoughts.

Afternoon light spilled across the cabin, glinting off surfaces as if catching on invisible threads. Ethan held out his hands, watching papers flutter lightly, pens rolling across the tabletop. The hum in the room rose in resonance with his heartbeat.

Hogan growled softly, crouched low, ears flattened. Ethan froze. The hum intensified. A candle flickered, the flame bending toward his hands as though drawn by gravity or thought. He stepped back, eyes wide, breath catching.

It was no longer small. The air was charged, alive. Objects reacted to his movement, subtle yet undeniable. The creek outside, normally silent, whispered along its banks, leaves shimmering faintly in rhythm with the thrum in the cabin.

Ethan felt the weight of his own disbelief pressing against him. He had tried to rationalize, explain it away. No longer. The world itself had responded to him.

Evening came with a softness that made the cabin shadows long and strange. Ethan leaned against the doorway, hands still tingling faintly, listening. Through the subtle hum, a faint whisper threaded its way in, almost beneath perception.

"Four more..."

He froze. The words weren't in any language he recognized, yet resonated in some primal corner of his mind. *Four more conduits.*

Hogan barked once, a sharp sound that echoed, as though acknowledging the presence of something beyond. Ethan's pulse spiked. Awe, fear, and something like reverence gripped him.

The whispers faded. Only the hum remained, steady, as if the house itself were breathing. He shivered.

Lila's presence had never felt closer, though she wasn't physically there yet. He could feel her heartbeat across the room, faint but undeniable. It was a thread, an extension of the energy flowing through him. He pressed a palm against his chest and felt the rhythm, mirrored faintly, coaxed from afar by proximity and connection.

Hogan crept over to Ethan's side, nudging him gently, then settling at his feet. The dog's warmth grounded him, a tether in the escalating, intangible chaos of power.

He wondered how this thread to Lila could exist without touch, without sight. He flexed his fingers experimentally, sending a faint pulse of life toward the dog. Hogan's fur shimmered in response. A small miracle.

By nightfall, Ethan had settled into a cautious routine. He experimented in measured pulses: a plant revived, Hogan brightened, small items suspended for brief instants. Each attempt honed his awareness of flow, direction, limits.

Energy coursed through him in pulses, sometimes fast, sometimes slow, tethered by intention and thought. Hogan responded instantly to the changes, tail wagging, paws kneading at the floor, intuitive. Ethan realized the reciprocity was as natural as breathing, life moving through him, not just from him.

He leaned back against the wall, Hogan resting against his side. The hum in the cabin persisted, subtle, resonant, alive. The creek's whisper outside matched it faintly, as though the natural world was acknowledging him, urging him to understand.

Ethan moved to the window, gazing out over the creek and surrounding woods. The air seemed charged, alive. Leaves rustled without wind, subtle flickers of light traced patterns along the underbrush. He exhaled slowly.

A notion seized him: *It's not just me.* Four others. The Weave. The world was threaded with energy, pulses moving, connections forming. The stakes were no longer personal, they were global, vast, impossible.

Hogan lifted his head, ears forward. The dog's gaze swept the woods, alert. Ethan felt the hum extend outward, brushing the edges of perception. He was a node in a network, tethered to something enormous and terrifying.

Ethan sank to the floor, legs crossed, hands hovering above a small plant. He let the pulse move freely, letting energy flow, accepting the give and take without restraint. The hum became richer, deeper, resonant.

Hogan lay beside him, head resting lightly against Ethan's arm. His eyes half-closed, he exhaled softly, syncing in some instinctual way. Ethan felt the rhythm, the exchange, the connection.

He realized he had surrendered, not out of defeat, but necessity. Control came not from suppression, but acknowledgment.

Night deepened, and the cabin became a vessel of quiet energy. The hum pulsed, faint glow along walls and floorboards tracing the unseen currents. Hogan slept at Ethan's feet. Outside, the creek glimmered faintly, a mirror to the unseen Weave.

Lila's presence was a memory and a thread. Ethan pressed his hands lightly against the floor, feeling the pulse of the world beneath him. His heartbeat synced faintly with the hum, with Hogan, with the thread that linked him to others he had not yet met.

For the first time, he did not flinch. Awe and dread coexisted, but there was clarity in the chaos. He was a conduit. A single point of life in a vast web.

And for the first time, he felt the weight and wonder of it all without fear paralyzing him.

The Weave hummed quietly, a rhythm beneath the world, waiting, responding, watching.

Hogan stirred, raising his head, and the dog's eyes reflected faint pulses of energy moving through the cabin. Ethan exhaled, steady, aware. The world had shifted, and he was at its center.

18

Collapse

The rain had been falling for hours before Ethan realized it wasn't normal rain.

It didn't sound right.

It hissed against the tin roof in erratic bursts, like static tearing through the night. The world beyond the cabin windows was a blur of wind and lightning, trees bending like they were bowing to something vast and unseen.

Ethan stood in the doorway, watching the treeline shudder. His shirt clung to him with sweat despite the chill. Hogan prowled back and forth near his boots, hackles up, every few seconds releasing a low growl that vibrated against the floorboards.

The Weave thrummed inside him, deep and wrong, an itch under the skin. Every flash of lightning seemed to echo in his bones, like his heartbeat and the storm had synced without his permission.

"Easy," he muttered to the dog. His voice came out hoarse. "It's just a storm."

But it wasn't.

The air inside the cabin smelled charged, ozone and woodsmoke. The lights flickered again, the generator stuttering somewhere out back. Ethan rubbed his palms together, then froze when he saw it: faint blue light pulsing in the lines of his veins.

No. Not again.

He stumbled to the sink, turned on the tap, splashed cold water on his face. The reflection in the window stared back pale and drawn, eyes too bright, the irises catching light even in the dark.

The hum got louder.

Outside, thunder broke like artillery. A tree split somewhere close, the shockwave rattling dishes in the cabinet. Hogan barked once, sharp, alarmed, then whimpered, retreating beneath the table.

Ethan gripped the counter. *Keep it down. Breathe.*
The Weave responded anyway, swelling under his skin, a current searching for ground.

Lightning forked across the sky, white fire illuminating the fields. For an instant, he saw something in the rain: faint threads of light, spiderwebbing through the air, vanishing as quickly as they appeared.

His pulse surged.

"Not now," he whispered. "Please, not now."

But the storm didn't care. The wind howled harder, the lights flickered again, then went black.

Silence.

Then, a low, resonant hum filled the cabin, not from the generator or the storm, but from *him.*

Ethan staggered back, breath ragged. Every nerve felt raw, electric. He could feel the lines, invisible but real, stretching outward from his body into the night, connecting to something vast. The world pulsed.

He gritted his teeth. "Stop,"
A flash, the world went white.

Outside, the barn roof exploded in a sheet of flame and splintering wood. The sound hit a heartbeat later, shaking the ground. Hogan yelped and bolted behind the couch.

Ethan hit his knees, clutching his temples. His vision fragmented, light, color, sensation. He *felt* the storm screaming in frequencies no ear should register.

The Weave wanted out.

He crawled to the door, dragging himself upright. The yard was chaos, wind thrashing through the grass, rain slanting sideways, lightning stabbing down into the fields again and again like it was targeting him.

Blue light arced from his fingers when he reached for the doorframe. Wood blackened, smoke curling upward.

"Oh, God."

He backed away, shaking his hand. The veins glowed again, brighter this time. The light wasn't just *inside* him, it was leaking out.

The wind howled louder, a voice without language, pressing against the cabin's walls until they creaked like bones about to break.

Ethan stumbled back from the door, heart hammering in his chest. Every instinct screamed to run, but where? The storm was everywhere. He could feel it, not just the sound or the motion of air, but the *pattern* underneath it, a living geometry twisting through the atmosphere.

He grabbed the flashlight from the counter, thumbed it on. The beam flickered blue, then died.

Static filled the air. His skin crawled.

He moved to the window, glass streaked with water, lightning flashing beyond. The yard was alive with motion. Trees bent low, their branches like skeletal arms clawing at the sky. But between the bolts of lightning, there was something else, faint, shifting figures, like silhouettes walking in the rain.

He blinked hard. They were gone.

Hogan barked once from under the table, a deep, fearful bark, then whined, ears pinned flat.

"Okay, okay," Ethan breathed. "We're fine. We're fine."

Another flash.

The world went *silent*.

No thunder. No wind. Just a pulse. Slow. Deep.

It came from beneath him, the ground itself. The boards under his bare feet trembled. A low, thrumming vibration climbed up his legs, into his spine, up behind his eyes. His teeth ached.

He gasped and dropped the flashlight. It rolled under the counter, useless.

Then came the heat.

It started in his chest, that same burning core that had ignited at the lake, only now it wasn't contained. His breath hitched; light leaked from the corners of his eyes. Every nerve in his body screamed. He stumbled backward, knocking into the table.

Hogan yelped and bolted.

The hum became a roar, a living circuit screaming for release.

Ethan staggered toward the door, flung it open. Rain slapped him across the face, cold and stinging. He stumbled out into the storm barefoot, the mud sucking at his feet. His shirt clung to his skin, soaked, the light under his flesh pulsing brighter now, steady with his heartbeat.

The sky tore open.

Bolts of lightning struck the field around him in perfect rhythm, not random, but *patterned*. They hit in concentric circles, one after another, until the ground itself was burning blue.

He screamed, falling to his knees. His palms slammed into the wet grass, and light erupted outward, webbing across the earth. The Weave came alive.

Lines of light burned into the mud, connecting to the trees, the fences, the creek beyond. The air shimmered like water, the smell of ozone thick enough to taste.

Ethan couldn't breathe. His chest felt like it would split open.

He looked up, and for a heartbeat, he saw the structure behind the world. The Weave itself, visible through the rain: billions of filaments stretching into infinity, each pulsing with some alien rhythm.

He reached toward it without meaning to.

And the world *answered*.

The field exploded with light.

A shockwave flattened the trees, sent mud and debris flying. Windows shattered in the cabin. The barn collapsed inward with a groan. Ethan was thrown backward, hit the ground hard enough to see stars.

He tried to move, but his limbs wouldn't obey. He could hear the Weave, not as sound, but as a vibration deep in his skull. A chorus of frequencies, overlapping, ancient.

Then, silence.

Rain fell softly again, hissing on the smoldering earth.

He rolled onto his side, groaning, chest heaving. The glow beneath his skin had dimmed but not gone. Every nerve still buzzed, the storm echoing inside him even as the real one passed overhead.

Hogan crawled toward him through the mud, tail low, whining. Ethan reached out weakly, resting a trembling hand on the dog's head. "It's... okay, buddy," he murmured, voice shredded. "We're still here."

A flicker of light rippled across the creek. The water glowed faintly blue, a mirror of the veins still alight beneath Ethan's skin.

He stared at it, rain running into his eyes.

Then headlights cut through the storm.

He turned his head weakly toward the road, a pair of government SUVs grinding up the muddy drive, their light bars off but engines loud. Shadows moved inside.

Hogan's growl deepened.

Ethan tried to push himself up, but his body wouldn't cooperate. His hands shook uncontrollably, his vision doubling. The light in his veins flickered with his heartbeat, visible even through the rain.

Doors slammed. Boots hit mud. Shouted voices.

"Federal agents! Stay where you are!"

Ethan coughed, the taste of blood on his tongue. He tried to raise a hand, to warn them, *Don't come close.*

But it was too late.

One agent reached him first, crouching low. "He's alive! We've got him!"

The man's hand brushed Ethan's arm.

A surge.

The agent convulsed, thrown backward into the mud, eyes wide. His body trembled violently before going limp. Another shouted for a medic. Two more approached, weapons drawn.

Ethan's vision blurred. The rain turned to streaks of white light.

"Don't," he tried to say. But his voice was gone.

A sting hit his neck, dart. Sedative. Cold flood.

The world began to fold inward. The thunder became muffled, distant, like he was hearing it through water.

He looked down at his hands one last time. The light was fading, retreating into his skin.

Then darkness closed around him.

The first thing Ethan felt was *cold.*

Not the clean, biting cold of rain, but chemical. Sterile. A chill that lived under his skin, crawling through his veins like frostbite. His eyelids were heavy, stuck halfway between open and closed.

Sound came in fragments, boots striking pavement, the low hum of an engine, someone shouting for medical clearance.

He tried to speak, but his tongue felt like lead.

Something jabbed his arm. Another surge of cold spread outward.

Then, silence again.

His thoughts blurred into shapes and color. Flashes. The storm. Blue light. Hogan's bark. Men shouting. The tranquilizer dart glinting in the lightning before it hit.

Now, darkness.

A voice floated through the fog, calm, professional, with a hint of an accent. *"Keep him restrained. No direct contact until we know what he is."*

That voice, familiar. Ramirez.

The back of the DHS transport rattled like a tin drum. Rain hammered the roof, streaking across the narrow windows. The air smelled of antiseptic and ozone.

Ramirez sat across from the containment cot; hands folded around a tablet glowing faint blue in the dim light.

Inside the restraint harness, Ethan Moore barely looked human, skin pallid, veins still faintly luminous under the surface. Electrodes traced the line of his arms, readings spiking every few seconds.

The bio-monitors made no sense. Heart rate irregular. Core temperature unstable. Cellular activity off the charts.

Ramirez frowned, scrolling through the telemetry. "You ever seen anything like this?" he asked the medic seated beside him.

The medic shook his head. "No trauma, no drugs. He should be in cardiac arrest with this much neural activity. But he's... holding steady."

Ramirez studied Ethan's face. The man looked younger like this, the hard edges softened by sedation. The faint pulse of light under his skin flickered in time with the vehicle's low hum.

"Jesus," one of the soldiers muttered near the door. "What the hell is he?"

Ramirez didn't answer. He didn't know.

He'd watched the same storm footage as everyone else, power grid surges across half the state, satellite imagery showing concentric EMP rings centered on a single location: Woodlawn, Tennessee. The eye of the storm.

And now here he was, breathing, heart still beating, the supposed *Miracle Medic.*

"Keep the restraints charged," Ramirez said quietly. "If he wakes up, I want a ten-meter distance between him and anyone breathing."

The medic hesitated. "You think he's dangerous?"

Ramirez looked back at the faint glow in Ethan's chest. "I think the laws of physics are starting to take him personally."

He drifted in and out, the sedative pulling him like undertow. The vibration of the vehicle hummed through the metal floor, syncing with the residual throb inside his ribs.

A voice, muffled but firm, spoke above him. He couldn't make out the words, only the rhythm.

He tried to open his eyes.

Light. White. The ceiling blurred. Shapes moving beyond it. A steady beep.

His fingers twitched against the restraints. He couldn't feel the leather, just pressure, distant and soft, like touching something underwater.

He thought of Lila, her voice in the rain, calling his name. He'd tried to answer. He wasn't sure if he had.

Then another voice reached him, deeper, almost inaudible, threading through the machinery hum.

"Ethan..."

He froze. The sound wasn't coming from outside. It was *inside*.

Kemen.

"You cannot cage what is returning."

The restraints vibrated. The ECG spiked.

Ramirez looked up from his tablet. "What the hell,?"

The lights flickered overhead.

Every screen in the van glitched, white static crawling across the monitors. A low hum filled the air, same frequency as the storm.

"Shut it down!" Ramirez barked.

Too late.

Blue light bled from Ethan's skin, faint, ghostly, pulsing through the restraints. The air crackled with static. A gust of cold wind, impossible inside the van, swept through the compartment.

Ethan's eyes opened.

For a heartbeat, they were white, no iris, no pupil.

Then he gasped, a deep, ragged inhale, and the glow vanished. His body went limp.

The monitors flatlined for two seconds. Then a weak rhythm returned.

Ramirez exhaled slowly. "Jesus Christ."

The medic whispered, "Sir, that wasn't a seizure."

"No," Ramirez said, staring at Ethan. "That was a warning."

By the time they reached the blacksite facility two hours later, the rain had stopped. The air outside was still heavy with static, like the storm hadn't ended, only paused.

Floodlights illuminated the concrete structure ahead. Security teams stood waiting, silhouettes under umbrellas, weapons low but ready.

The van doors opened with a hiss.

"Subject secure," Ramirez called out. "Vitals irregular but stable."

Two med techs wheeled the cot out, moving quickly toward the facility doors. Ramirez followed, the smell of ozone lingering in the air.

Above them, lightning flickered silently across a cloudless sky.

He looked up, uneasy.

For the briefest instant, he swore he saw it, faint and vast, stretching from horizon to horizon: the same *circle with five intersecting lines,* glowing high in the atmosphere before fading into nothing.

Ramirez whispered to himself, "What the hell are we waking up?"

When Ethan woke again, there was no rain.

No wind.

No sound.

Just the slow, artificial rhythm of a machine breathing for him.

A ceiling light burned white overhead , cold, sterile, wrong. He blinked against it, disoriented. The air felt too clean, too still. There was no scent of wood smoke or wet earth, only disinfectant and electricity.

He tried to move. His body didn't respond.

A soft *beep* echoed beside him. A heart monitor. He turned his head slightly. Clear tubing trailed from his arm. Electrodes dotted his chest. The faint hum of fluorescent lights vibrated through his skull.

He wasn't home.

Memory returned in fragments, the storm, the light, the dart. Then darkness.

Now this.

He was restrained again, wrists and ankles secured to the bed with wide gray straps. The room around him was windowless, its walls seamless steel. Cameras in two corners. One door. No sound from beyond it.

A faint crackle whispered through the air vents, static, like a radio off-station.

He froze, heart rate spiking.

"Kemen?" he whispered, the word scraping his throat raw.

No answer.

He waited.

Nothing.

The silence pressed harder, heavier than any storm.

He closed his eyes, trying to feel for the pulse, that low hum of energy that had always lingered in his chest since the Weave awoke inside him. But now, there was... almost nothing. Like static after a channel's gone dead.

They'd caged it.

Caged *him*.

A hiss, airlock cycling. The door opened.

Three people entered: two guards in tactical black and a woman in a lab coat with a tablet in her hands. She didn't look at him at first.

"Vitals are within acceptable ranges," she said. Her voice was clipped, efficient. "Temperature's dropped another degree. Neural activity down by forty percent."

The taller guard shifted uneasily. "You sure he's out?"

"Sedation should last another hour. Unless..."

Ethan's fingers twitched.

Her head snapped up. Their eyes met.

For a heartbeat, neither moved.

The air between them hummed, faint, almost inaudible, but enough to make the nearest monitor flicker.

"Jesus," she breathed.

The guards stepped forward, hands on their weapons.

Ethan coughed, dry, painful. "Where... where am I?"

"Don't speak," the woman said sharply, though her voice trembled. "You need to stay calm."

"Where am I?" His voice came stronger this time, more grounded.

The woman hesitated. "You're at a federal containment facility. You were found during... an anomalous weather event."

He almost laughed. It came out as a rasp. "That what you call it?"

The monitors flickered again, numbers stuttering. One of the guards cursed under his breath.

"Doc," the other said, "something's,"

Every light in the room went out.

Silence.

Then the machines started humming, softly at first, then louder, the pitch rising like feedback. The heart monitor beside the bed pulsed blue instead of green.

The doctor took a step back, fear flickering across her face. "He's interacting with the power grid."

Ethan's body tensed against the restraints. He could feel it, electricity crawling through the room, drawn to him, through him. Not violent this time. Not wild. Just *there*, recognizing him.

He whispered, barely audible, "I didn't mean to..."

A soft ping sounded from the doctor's tablet. She glanced down. The screen was white noise, static crawling across it like frost.

Then, faintly, words began to form in the static lines.

THE CIRCLE FRAYS.

The doctor gasped and dropped the tablet. It clattered to the floor, the words fading instantly.

"What the hell was that?" one guard demanded.

"I, I don't know," she said, backing toward the door. "It's not from the system."

The hum in the air deepened. Ethan could feel it in his teeth now, in his heartbeat. It was the Weave, trying to push through the concrete, the steel, the sedatives.

The guards grabbed her arms. "We're getting you out,"

But then, just as quickly as it had started, everything went still. The lights blinked back on. The machines returned to normal.

Ethan's head dropped back to the pillow, drained. His breathing slowed.

The woman stared at him for a long moment, eyes wide, then whispered, almost to herself, "What are you?"

Ethan didn't answer.

He wasn't sure anymore.

From the security control room, Agent Cole Ramirez watched the scene unfold on a wall of monitors. He'd seen strange things in twenty years of federal work, but nothing like this.

The playback feed showed data streams spiking off the charts, the power flicker radiating outward in concentric rings. And for three full seconds, every digital system in the building had registered the same anomaly:

Circle with five intersecting lines.

No source. No signal origin.

Ramirez leaned forward. "Pause it."

The tech froze the frame.

It was faint, but visible, hovering above Ethan's body like an afterimage burned into film.

Five lines converging in a circle. Five points, each pulsing in sequence.

"What does it mean?" the tech asked quietly.

Ramirez didn't answer right away. He just stared at the frozen image.

"I think," he said finally, "it means he's not the only one."

Ethan lay in the sterile light, eyes half-open, barely conscious.

The faint blue glow beneath his skin flickered once, then steadied, rhythmic again, like a heartbeat syncing with something far larger than himself.

Outside, a low rumble of thunder rolled across the horizon, clear sky above the facility.

And somewhere deep inside the electrical grid, unseen, five faint pulses moved in perfect unison.

19

Capture

Light. Too white. Too still.

Ethan woke to the sound of humming, a low, endless vibration that didn't belong to any storm or machine he recognized. It filled the room like a thought you couldn't shake. The ceiling above him was sterile metal, perfectly smooth, without seams or bolts. No windows. No natural light. Just the constant, pulsing hum.

His throat was dry. He tried to swallow but couldn't. Something tugged at his arm. He turned his head and saw the IV line taped to his skin, the pale green fluid dripping into his vein.

He wasn't home.

The restraints were softer this time, padded, but just as firm. His wrists and ankles were bound to a reclined metal chair, angled upright like a crucifix laid halfway flat. He couldn't move more than a few inches either way.

He exhaled slowly, the air sharp with antiseptic.

Hospital, he thought first. But hospitals didn't hum like this. Hospitals didn't smell like ozone and refrigeration.

A voice cut through the stillness, tinny and distant through a speaker overhead.

"Subject 1A3 is awake."

He blinked hard. There was a faint click, then the sound of a door seal disengaging. Figures entered the room, three in lab coats, one in tactical black. They moved with clinical precision, gloved hands hovering over equipment.

The nearest scientist, a tall man with silver hair and glasses, spoke into a headset. "Vitals stable. Neural activity elevated. Cortisol at 340 nanograms per milliliter, elevated but consistent with acute stress response."

The words rolled over him like a wave of static. Ethan's mind struggled to latch onto anything familiar. He focused on his breathing. *Four seconds in. Hold. Four seconds out.*

"Can you hear me?" the man asked.

Ethan nodded weakly. "Where am I?"

The scientist didn't answer right away. Instead, he adjusted a monitor, then muttered to a colleague, "Regenerative baseline holding. Increase luminal output by two."

The overhead lights intensified. Ethan flinched.

"Where," he croaked, ", am I?"

"Federal containment facility," the man replied at last, not looking at him. "We're just running a few tests."

He turned to one of the monitors. The screens were filled with color-coded graphs, red, blue, white. One of them displayed an outline of Ethan's body, pulsing faintly with blue light. It looked like heat vision, but colder.

Something stirred in his chest. Not emotion, energy. The hum in the room synced with his heartbeat for a split second, then fell out of rhythm. The lights flickered.

"Did you see that?" one of the scientists whispered.

The lead doctor, Halvorsen, according to his badge, frowned. "Electrical interference. Check the grounding."

Ethan swallowed again, voice hoarse. "That wasn't interference."

No one answered.

Hours bled together, or maybe minutes. Ethan couldn't tell. They drew blood, took scans, injected something that burned through his veins like frost. He felt every heartbeat echo through him as though the world itself had a pulse.

The machines reacted. Monitors flickered. Data scrambled, re-assembled, vanished.

He watched his own wounds close in real time, shallow scratches on his forearm from the restraints sealing shut under the fluorescent glare. A murmur rippled through the lab.

"Regeneration rate exceeds measurable threshold."

"Impossible."

"Not impossible," Halvorsen said quietly. "Just undocumented."

The hum in the air grew stronger. Ethan could feel it brushing the edge of consciousness, threads of sound, faint and layered, whispering beneath the mechanical drone. He focused on one, almost human in tone.

Ethan.

He froze. His eyes darted around the room, but no one had spoken. The whisper faded as quickly as it came.

He closed his eyes. When he opened them again, faint filaments of light danced in the air, invisible to the others. They curved, weaving between the scientists, trailing from their hands, their hearts. The Weave.

He breathed, careful not to show reaction.

The woman at the next console, Dr. Merrin, looked uneasy. "This isn't right. The readings change when he focuses."

Halvorsen ignored her. "Increase EM field by five percent."

The hum deepened. The filaments brightened.

"Stop," Ethan said.

"Relax, Mr. Moore."

"Stop." His voice rose, something ancient curling beneath it.

Every screen in the room went black. Then filled with static.

For three seconds, the noise formed a pattern, a perfect circle intersected by five glowing lines. Each line ended in a faint rune.

The staff froze.

Then the screens blinked to normal again, as if nothing had happened.

"Cut power," Halvorsen barked.

Too late.

Ethan's pulse flared, a visible ripple beneath his skin, veins glowing faintly blue before fading again.

Merrin whispered, "My God."

He met her eyes. "He's not listening to you."

Upstairs, behind three inches of ballistic glass, Agent Cole Ramirez watched the feed with his hands locked behind his back.

He'd spent two weeks on this case, long enough to know when people were lying. Ethan Moore wasn't. Whatever this was, he wasn't faking it.

The feed replayed in slow motion: every camera flickering to static, the brief flash of the circle symbol, the way Moore's vitals spiked and stabilized again.

Ramirez exhaled slowly. "You think he's dangerous?"

His superior, Director Cavanaugh, didn't look up from her notes. "I think he's a potential energy weapon. Whether he wants to be or not doesn't matter."

"That's not what I asked."

"You've seen the reports. He revived a dead child. He's linked to three regional blackouts. I don't need a moral assessment, Agent."

Ramirez clenched his jaw. "He's a person, ma'am. Not a reactor."

She finally looked up. "That depends on whether he stays human."

She left the room. Ramirez stared after her, then turned back to the monitors. Ethan sat motionless, head bowed, the faintest shimmer of light pulsing from his chest in slow rhythm.

Something about it unsettled him, not because it looked dangerous, but because it looked... sacred.

They sedated him again that night.

He drifted under, not into sleep but into something deeper. The hum followed him.

When he opened his eyes, he wasn't in the lab anymore.

He stood on a vast lattice of light, a glowing web stretched across a darkened Earth. Each filament shimmered like starlight, threading through oceans and mountains, cities and hearts. The Weave.

Kemen stood before him. Her eyes burned gold.

"The world's pulse is fading," she said softly. "You are its heartbeat."

Ethan shook his head. "No. I didn't ask for this."

"Neither did we," she said. "But the seal weakens. And the silence we held for twenty millennia cracks."

He looked down. The Weave rippled beneath his feet, millions of connections dimming, flickering, dying.

"Stop it," he whispered.

"You can't. Only balance it."

Her hand lifted. "Five hands. One for each path. Yours burns first."

Light bloomed across the sky, five lines intersecting in a circle, four blazing white-blue, one still black and lifeless.

"What does it mean?" he asked.

"That the world is remembering. And that memory comes with a cost."

She touched his chest. Pain ignited. A rune seared into his skin, lines of light radiating outward, then burning away.

Ethan gasped, falling backward, into darkness, into the hum.

He woke screaming.

The restraints were gone. Or maybe broken. The lights flickered overhead. Alarms howled in distant corridors.

He sat upright, chest heaving, heart hammering.

The room was scorched around him, faint spirals of soot on the walls, like fingerprints from a divine hand.

He looked down.

Through the tatters of his hospital gown, a faint blue light pulsed under his skin. Lines spread outward from the center of his chest, five thin paths, intersecting in a circle. Four glowed. One remained dark.

He touched it, trembling. The light faded under his fingertips, then returned, slow and steady, a heartbeat not entirely his own.

Beyond the one-way glass, Ramirez stood frozen, staring at the monitor.

"What is that?" the tech whispered.

Ramirez couldn't answer. He could only stare at the symbol hovering faintly over Ethan's body, perfectly formed, luminous and impossible.

He felt a chill crawl up his spine, the instinctive sense that whatever was happening inside that cell wasn't *contained* at all.

Ethan looked up, eyes distant, voice calm and terrifyingly sure.

"It's not me," he said. "It's waking up."

20

Breakout

The hum was wrong.

It started low, deep in the concrete, too deep to belong to the generators. It rose in waves, like something enormous breathing beneath the building. Lights pulsed once, twice, then steadied, but the rhythm stayed.

A heartbeat.

Ethan stirred on the cot. The restraints had been loosened since the last test, though his arms still ached from where they'd been fixed to the chair. A thin medical monitor beeped beside him, trying to match his pulse but falling out of sync. He turned his head toward the mirrored glass.

No movement. No one watching.

Except there was. He could feel them. Their attention crawled along his skin like static.

He sat up, wincing as the IV tugged at his arm. His breath came slow and deliberate, the kind of breathing he used to survive firefights and panic attacks alike. The air in the cell felt heavier now, pressurized. The hum thickened until he could feel it under his ribs.

The ceiling light flickered.

"Not again," he muttered.

Across the observation room, Ramirez watched the monitor feeds. His coffee was cold, untouched for hours. He'd been up since the night before, eyes raw, waiting for orders from Washington. The other agents had rotated out. He hadn't.

The readings didn't make sense. Every time Ethan's vitals spiked, the magnetic field in the containment wing bent by a measurable degree, like gravity itself warped to follow the man's breathing.

"System error?" one of the technicians asked.

Ramirez didn't answer. He leaned forward, elbows on his knees, staring through the glass.

Inside, Ethan rubbed his temples, muttering to himself. His voice carried, low but clear:
"You can't hold it. You can't,"
The lights blinked out.
Then came back on.
Then dimmed again, pulsing faintly blue.
Ramirez's headset crackled. "Agent Ramirez, containment systems are drawing power from unregistered nodes. We're reading surges across," The voice cut off in a burst of static.

Ethan froze. He could hear the building groaning, the same way the earth groaned before a quake. A faint scent of ozone filled the air, sharp and metallic.

He closed his eyes, tried to steady himself. *Stay calm. Stay centered.*
But the hum climbed higher.
It wasn't just in the walls, it was inside him now.
The light changed.
At first, it was just a faint shimmer crawling across the floor tiles, like water reflecting something unseen above. Then it rose in thin filaments, hovering midair. Blue-white threads wove through the room, brushing his skin, luminous and alive.

Ethan took a step back. "No," he whispered. "Not here."

The IV pole rattled. Metal screws vibrated loose, floating for a heartbeat before clattering to the floor.

He backed against the wall, pressing his palms to the cold tile. The hum filled his chest cavity, every heartbeat a drum against the storm of sound.

"Calm down," he whispered. "You're not a reactor. You're not,"

The wall lit up under his hands.

It flared with the same light as the Weave, veins of blue streaking outward from his fingertips. His pulse accelerated. The hum synchronized. For one impossible moment, everything, heart, current, gravity, aligned.

Then the room exploded in light.

Ramirez shielded his eyes as the containment glass flashed white. The feed went to static across every monitor.

"Kill power to the sector!" someone shouted.

"Main breakers aren't responding!"

Sparks rained from ceiling panels. The floor shook. Emergency lights flickered on in crimson bars along the walls. Ramirez stumbled toward the viewing window.

Through the static, through the fractured glass, he saw Ethan standing in the epicenter of it all, barefoot, head tilted upward, light crawling along his skin in streams of luminescent blue. The restraints had melted away like wax.

"Jesus," Ramirez whispered.

The agents beside him aimed rifles through the reinforced glass. "Orders?"

"Hold your fire," Ramirez snapped.

But it was already too late.

The hum became a roar. Every electronic device in the lab detonated in synchronized bursts, blooming into silent arcs of blue flame. The flames didn't consume, they froze, hanging midair, like trapped aurora.

Ethan screamed. It wasn't pain exactly, it was overflow.

The air trembled. The walls warped. The Weave pressed through the fabric of matter, visible to him and him alone, a web of radiant threads connecting every molecule, every life.

It was too much. Too much.

He reached out, fingers trembling, and the world bent to his touch.

Containment didn't fail.

It dissolved.

The reinforced steel folded outward like rippling water, and the air flooded with radiance. Sirens went silent, their sound swallowed by light. Time slowed, not illusion, not metaphor, but literal compression of motion.

Guards in the corridor froze mid-run, bullets hanging motionless in the air. Droplets of water from a ruptured pipe shimmered like suspended glass beads.

Ethan stepped forward. Each footfall left faint glowing impressions on the tile that faded seconds after he passed.

He could hear everything, the breathing of unconscious technicians, the faint thump of their hearts. Life sang to him in thousands of overlapping notes.

"I didn't mean," His voice broke. "I didn't mean this."

He tried to stop it, to shut himself down, but the Weave had no off switch. It flowed *through* him, not *from* him.

Ramirez stumbled through the haze, coughing as the air thickened. "Ethan! You have to,"

The words died as he saw the expression on the man's face.

Not rage. Not madness. Grief.

The Weave curved around Ramirez, sparing him. He felt the energy brush his skin, warm, soft, almost compassionate.

"Go," Ethan said, voice shaking. "Before it takes you too."

Ramirez hesitated. "They'll say you killed them."

"Then let them. But you know better."

Their eyes met. The blue light between them pulsed once, and the agent stepped back as Ethan turned toward the outer wall.

He didn't move his hands. Didn't speak. The concrete simply peeled away, layer by layer, dissolving into cascading ribbons of aurora that flowed upward into the night.

The storm outside swallowed him whole.

Rain fell like absolution.

Ethan staggered across the field beyond the facility perimeter, barefoot, soaked, steam rising from his skin. The air smelled of iron and rain and ozone.

Behind him, the DHS complex glowed faintly, a collapsed skeleton wreathed in light.

He dropped to his knees in the mud. His hands trembled.

"I never wanted this," he whispered.

Lightning rolled across the sky, silent this time. The hum had quieted, reduced to a heartbeat somewhere beneath the thunder.

A low whine reached his ears.

Hogan.

The dog burst through the brush, caked in mud, tail wagging weakly. He pressed his muzzle into Ethan's lap, trembling.

Ethan buried a hand in the wet fur. "You found me."

The dog's chest vibrated with a small sound that wasn't quite a bark, wasn't quite a whimper.

"I can't go back, boy," Ethan murmured. "Not after this."

He looked up. Through the storm clouds, faint curtains of blue light shimmered, rippling like silk, aurora where none should exist.

The same light as the Weave.

It stretched horizon to horizon, vast and alive.

He felt it reach for him, then pull back, testing, waiting.

He closed his eyes. The rain slid down his face, cold and clean. For a moment, the hum within him matched the rhythm of the falling water.

When he opened his eyes again, the world was quiet.

Too quiet.

The kind of silence that comes after something divine has passed through and left the air too heavy for words.

He rose, shoulders slumped, Hogan pressed close to his side.

Every step left faint glowing impressions in the wet soil that faded with the rain.

Ethan and Hogan walked away from the burning facility under the rain, the aurora faint above the storm clouds, the rune glowing faintly through his soaked shirt, five lines, four bright, one still dark.

21

The Prophet's Warning

The chapel rose out of the trees like a ghost.

Ethan found it just before dawn, after hours of stumbling through the backroads and low fields that sloped away from the ruined DHS complex. The storm had burned itself out sometime after midnight, leaving a world washed raw, branches slick with rain, air sharp with ozone. His clothes clung to him, streaked with dried mud. Hogan walked a few steps behind, head low, ribs showing through wet fur.

The church wasn't much to look at. One room, stone and timber, its bell tower leaning sideways as if too tired to stand. The front doors hung crooked. He pushed one open, and the hinges cried out like something waking from a long sleep.

Inside, it smelled of wet wood and old dust. The kind of dust that doesn't gather in months but in decades. Moonlight, or maybe dawn-light, it was hard to tell which , slipped through broken stained glass, scattering colored shards across the warped floorboards. Rows of pews sat in uneven lines, a few tipped over, some half-rotted. The altar was cracked down the middle, the crucifix above it splintered but still standing.

Ethan stood in the doorway for a long time, dripping onto the warped wood. The wind outside hissed through the eaves, a slow, steady whisper. For a second, it almost sounded like his name again. He ignored it.

He crossed the aisle, boots squelching, and sank onto the nearest pew. Hogan followed, curling at his feet, sighing through his nose in that small, tired way dogs do when they've run too far.

Ethan rubbed his face with shaking hands. His palms felt fever-warm, as they had since the facility, faintly thrumming under the skin, like a current just beneath the surface. The hum had lessened, but it hadn't gone. Every few seconds, it pulsed, reminding him he wasn't free of it.

That he never would be.

He looked up at the cross. "You got a hell of a sense of humor," he muttered.

The silence answered. Not even birds yet. Just the faint drip of rain through the broken roof.

He stripped off his soaked shirt and dropped it beside him. The blue light beneath his sternum still glowed faintly, barely visible until the candlelight hit it, except there was no candlelight here. The glow came from him.

He stared down at it, exhausted. "You're gonna kill me, aren't you?" he whispered.

Hogan lifted his head, ears pricked, watching him.

Ethan leaned forward, elbows on his knees. "Should've let me burn out back there."

He felt the weight of the world pressing through his skull, the aftermath of the surge, of being too much vessel, not enough man. His veins still tingled. His heart beat slow but hard, each pulse echoing faintly through the pews around him. The rhythm matched the distant roll of thunder, far away now, heading east.

When he exhaled, a faint mist escaped his lips, though it wasn't cold inside. It was energy bleeding off him, almost invisible, rising like heat. He could see faint ripples around his fingers, as if the air itself bent.

He forced his hands still.

After a while, he pulled a matchbook from the breast pocket of his coat. Found it damp but usable. He lit one, touching it to the stub of a candle still stuck in a rusted holder near the altar.

The flame took, burning low at first, then stronger. Pale.
Not gold. Not red.
Blue-white.

He stared at it until the wax started to melt down the sides.

"Guess that answers that," he murmured.

He stayed like that through dawn, sitting in the pew, shirtless, hands folded between his knees. Hogan dozed and woke, dozed and woke again. The world outside brightened from gray to silver, and through a crack in the roof, a single beam of daylight spilled across the altar. It lit the crucifix like a promise, or maybe a warning.

Ethan shut his eyes.

He dreamed, but not deeply. Just flashes, light breaking through water, voices half-heard in static, a woman's eyes like molten gold. *The world's pulse is fading,* she whispered again. *You are its heartbeat.*
He woke with his teeth clenched and the candle half gone.

By late morning, the rain started again, softer this time, steady enough to fill the silence.

He thought about leaving. Heading north. Disappearing for good this time. But where would he go? Every camera, every rumor, every whisper online, the "Miracle Medic" story had burned through the world already. He could change his name, his face, but the thing inside him didn't care about names.

He leaned back against the pew, staring at the cracked ceiling. The wooden beams creaked softly, expanding in the damp. Hogan shifted and rested his muzzle on Ethan's boot.

"Don't look at me like that," Ethan said quietly. "You didn't sign up for this."

The dog's tail thumped once, slow.

Something inside him broke then, not with sound, not with pain, just the quiet ache of realizing how small the world had become. A man and a dog in a forgotten chapel, waiting for something neither of them could name.

He pressed his hand against his chest. The light pulsed faintly under his palm. "If you're listening," he whispered, eyes still closed, "make it stop."

The hum answered, soft, patient, infinite.

Not cruel.

Just there.

Ethan lowered his hand. "Yeah. That's what I thought."

Outside, a car engine cut through the sound of rain.

He sat up.

Ethan heard the crunch of tires first. Not fast, cautious, deliberate. A pickup, by the sound. Then the engine cut out, replaced by the hollow tick of cooling metal. Hogan's head came up before Ethan's did, the dog's ears twitched, a low growl coiling in his chest.

Ethan eased to his feet, every muscle tight. He reached for the old crowbar leaning against the pew, habit, not thought. The candlelight flickered with the motion. Through the warped panes of stained glass, he saw a figure step into the rain.

Tall, broad, with the stiff posture of someone used to command. A raincoat hung off his shoulders, the hood pushed back. The man's hair was thinner than Ethan remembered, grayer at the edges, but that walk, the measured, sure rhythm, he'd know anywhere.

"Easy," Ethan murmured to Hogan. The dog went silent but didn't relax.

The church door creaked open.

"I always told you," the man said quietly, "you'd end up running to the quiet places."

The voice hit like a round to the chest, familiar, heavy with the weight of old battlefields.

Ethan lowered the crowbar, but only slightly. "You following me now, Reverend?"

Samuel Tate stepped fully into the chapel, shutting the door behind him. He wasn't wearing a collar, just a dark shirt under the raincoat, jeans, boots scuffed with red clay. His eyes were the same, steady, assessing, the kind that could settle a platoon or a congregation.

"Didn't have to follow," Tate said, shaking rain from his sleeves. "You light up the sky these days."

Ethan managed half a smirk, though it didn't reach his eyes. "Guess I should've figured the church would send somebody."

"I didn't come on orders," Tate said. "I came because the radio in my truck started talking in your voice. Quoting scripture you don't even know."

Ethan blinked. "You expect me to believe that?"

"I don't much care what you believe anymore, son," Tate said, walking farther inside. "I just know the world's gone strange, and every road I take leads back to you."

They stood there in the half-light, rain tapping the roof, the silence between them filled with years they hadn't spoken. Hogan sniffed the air, uncertain, then padded to Tate's boots and sat. The reverend reached down, scratching his head.

"Still collecting strays," he said softly. "That tracks."

Ethan finally set the crowbar against the wall and sat again on the pew. "You drove all this way to check if I was possessed?"

Tate gave a small, humorless smile. "I drove because I remember a kid bleeding out on a mountainside in Afghanistan, cursing a God he didn't believe in. That same kid brought three others home alive. Figure if Heaven's paying attention, they might call in old debts."

Ethan leaned forward, elbows on his knees. "Don't preach at me."

"I'm not," Tate said, voice even. "I'm asking what happened."

Ethan hesitated. The candle sputtered, its flame thinning to a line of pale blue.

"You wouldn't believe me."

Tate sat across from him, the pew creaking under his weight. "Try me."

For a moment, Ethan didn't answer. The hum beneath his skin had steadied, quiet but constant, like a heartbeat he could hear through his bones. He looked up at the Reverend, saw the old scar on his jawline, the same one from Kandahar. Some wounds never faded; others, he guessed, did the opposite, they grew.

"It's not what you think," Ethan said finally. "It's not holy."

"Does it heal?"

"Yes."

"Then maybe it's not what *you* think either."

Ethan let out a low laugh, sharp and hollow. "You've got an answer for everything, don't you?"

"Not this time," Tate said. "But I do know this, things like what you're carrying don't show up for no reason."

"Then maybe it's a mistake," Ethan said. "God fat-fingered an order."

Tate didn't flinch. "You ever think He picked the only one who'd understand the cost?"

The words hit something raw. Ethan looked away. The rain was harder now, running down the cracked stained glass like tears. The candle threw long, fractured shadows across the walls.

"You came all this way," Ethan said quietly, "and you still don't get it. I'm not chosen. I'm a damn reactor that can't shut down."

"Maybe," Tate said, "but even a reactor gives light."

Ethan's laugh died before it reached his throat.

Tate studied him for a moment, then opened the worn leather satchel he carried. Inside were papers, photographs, a Bible so used its spine was nearly broken. He set them gently on the altar, beside the candle.

"You know what this place was called?" Tate asked.

Ethan shook his head.

"Saint Dymphna's. Patron saint of the broken." Tate smiled faintly. "Seemed fitting."

Ethan stared at the candle, its flame trembling in the draft. "You think I can fix something."

"I think maybe you already are," Tate said. "You just can't see it yet."

They sat in silence, listening to the rain on the roof. Hogan pressed against Ethan's leg, shivering once before settling. The air inside the chapel felt charged, alive, not just with static, but something subtler, older.

Ethan rubbed the back of his neck. "You feel that?"

"Feels like a storm that forgot to leave," Tate said. "Or maybe one that's waiting on us."

Ethan almost smiled. "You always did talk like a preacher."

"Better than talking like a ghost," Tate said. Then, after a pause: "You been seeing any?"

Ethan froze, eyes narrowing. "Why would you ask that?"

"Because the dead don't stay gone when something like this wakes up." Tate's tone softened. "And because I saw one in my church last week. Said your name."

Ethan looked at him, the silence long enough to make the air hum.

"Guess they're everywhere now," he said quietly.

Outside, thunder rolled again, low and distant. The candlelight wavered.

"Maybe," Tate said, "it's time to stop running from what's calling you."

Ethan met his eyes. "You think I'm supposed to answer it?"

"I think," Tate said, "you already have."

Tate unbuckled the worn satchel and drew out a bundle wrapped in oil-stained linen. He laid it on the altar beside the candle. The smell of the cloth was old, library dust and gun oil. When he peeled it back, thin papers and photographs slid into the light: a yellowed sketch of concentric circles crossed by five lines, old enough that the ink had bled to sepia.

Ethan stared.

"Where'd you get that?"

"Seminary archives first," Tate said. "Then a contact at Vanderbilt who collects apocrypha. You remember how I used to preach about the *Hands of Creation*?"

Ethan shook his head slowly. "I remember tuning you out."

"Well," Tate said with a faint smile, "you probably should've listened."

He smoothed the page flat. The symbol matched what Ethan had seen carved in light across his dreams, the same circle, the same five spokes ending in runes that seemed to breathe on the paper.

"This text is older than Scripture," Tate went on. "Fragments of something called the *Covenant of Renewal*. It talks about five who would return when the world's balance failed. Healers. Keepers. Fire-bearers. Each a piece of the Weave."

Ethan's throat felt dry. "The *Weave*," he said. "You don't even know what that means."

"Maybe not," Tate said, "but you do."

Ethan folded his arms, turning toward the broken stained-glass window. "I've been having dreams. Voices. Symbols like that one. Every time I think I'm losing it, something else happens. And now you're telling me there's a prophecy?"

Tate nodded. "Not a prophecy. A warning. Says the Five will come when the seal frays, when life and death stop keeping their distance." He looked up at Ethan. "You think that sounds like coincidence?"

Ethan wanted to scoff, but his stomach turned instead. The hum beneath his ribs answered with a small pulse. The blue light flashed through his shirt like a heartbeat caught in lightning.

Tate saw it and didn't flinch. "That's what I mean. The world's been bleeding dry for a long time, son. Maybe this is how it starts healing."

Ethan leaned his hands on the pew back, head down. "You call it healing. I call it a nightmare that doesn't end."

"You ever wonder why the nightmares started?" Tate asked. "Why men like us can't stop seeing what we saw over there?"

Ethan didn't answer.

"Maybe because something in you already knew how close the Weave was to tearing," Tate said softly. "You were built to hold it together."

Ethan's laugh came out cracked. "So now I'm what? God's duct tape?"

"If it keeps the world from falling apart, maybe that's enough," Tate said.

The words hung there a moment, the candle's blue flame reflected in his eyes. Hogan shifted, resting his head on Ethan's boot, sensing the charge that crept through the air.

Tate reached into the satchel again and produced a page torn from a different manuscript, its edges brittle as ash. On it, a handprint was pressed in some faded pigment, five marks radiating outward.

"Each hand," he said, "was tied to an element of creation, life, flame, wind, stone, and spirit. The texts say when they return, the circle remakes itself."

Ethan felt his pulse quicken. He remembered the dream, five points of light over the Earth, one dim, four burning. *One of five.*

"You think there are others?" he asked.

Tate nodded. "I think the others are waking up right now."

Ethan stared at the handprint until the edges blurred. For a heartbeat, it wasn't ink anymore, it moved, threads of faint light connecting the lines, weaving, pulsing.

He blinked hard and it was gone.

"This isn't faith," he said finally. "It's physics I don't understand."

"Faith is just physics we haven't named yet," Tate said. "And maybe you're the first man who's supposed to measure it."

Ethan turned toward him. "And if I don't want to?"

"Then the Weave will choose someone else," Tate said. "But I don't think it will. It's already anchored in you."

Ethan looked down at his hands, the faint glow in the veins, the tremor under his skin. "Anchored," he repeated. "Feels more like chained."

Tate sighed. "Chains hold a bridge together too."

For a long while, the only sound was the rain drumming steady on the roof. The candle had burned low, its wax pooling blue on the altar. Tate began to gather his papers, sliding them back into the satchel. Ethan kept watching the symbol, half expecting it to move again.

When Tate straightened, he said quietly, "I don't know what this means for you, Ethan. But every war needs a medic."

Ethan looked up, eyes hollow. "And every medic ends up covered in blood."

Tate hesitated, then closed the satchel. "Maybe this time, it's supposed to be different."

Outside, thunder rolled far off toward the horizon. Hogan lifted his head, whining once. The candle guttered, flared, then steadied again, blue light caught between breath and prayer.

The rain came back with a low whisper, brushing across the roof like fingertips. Each drop sounded heavier than the last, soft, deliberate, almost reverent. The candle on the altar guttered, recovered, then leaned with the draft.

Ethan sat motionless on the pew, eyes fixed on the warped floorboards. His jaw was tight, the muscles jumping like he was clenching against something too big to hold. Tate lingered near the altar, silent, letting the storm speak in his place.

When Ethan finally spoke, his voice was low and hoarse. "Then why does it hurt to heal?"

Tate looked up.

Ethan's hands were trembling in his lap, palms open, raw with half-healed cuts. "Every time I bring something back... I *feel it* go through me. Not just them breathing again. Everything. Their pain, their last thought, the *fear*." He swallowed hard. "And when they die, I feel that too. Like something gets ripped out of me."

His voice cracked. "Why? Why would it work like that?"

Tate took a slow step forward. "Because creation hurts," he said softly. "Always has."

Ethan shook his head, laughing once, bitter and quiet. "You make it sound noble."

"It's not noble," Tate said. He came closer, kneeling beside him. "It's the cost. Every miracle's got one. You just happen to know the price better than most."

Ethan dragged his hands over his face. His skin was hot, feverish. The air around them buzzed faintly, as though the chapel had begun to breathe. Blue light pulsed in time with his heartbeat, seeping from his chest, glancing off the wet wood.

The rain thickened outside, hitting the roof in uneven waves. Somewhere above, thunder rolled, low, patient, like an answer that didn't need to hurry.

Ethan whispered, "I didn't ask for this."

"I don't think you were asked," Tate said. "I think you were *needed*."

Ethan laughed again, sharper this time. "Needed. You think God looks down, sees the broken ones, and says 'That'll do'?"

Tate didn't move. "Maybe that's exactly who He picks. Because the ones who break know how not to."

The silence stretched.

Hogan lifted his head, ears twitching at something unseen. The dog's eyes caught the candlelight, reflecting faint blue, same hue as the glow beneath Ethan's ribs. The hum grew stronger, a low vibration in the air.

Ethan looked up, breathing hard. The stained glass, what was left of it, had begun to shimmer. The old shards embedded in the frame pulsed with a faint luminescence, colors shifting through dull blues and ghostly golds. The overcast sky outside should have choked the light, but somehow it spilled through brighter than the sun.

"What's happening?" he whispered.

Tate glanced toward the window. "I think you're listening," he said.

Ethan's tears started then, soundless at first. They slipped down his face, falling to the warped boards between his boots. Each drop landed, spread, and for an instant, just one heartbeat, glowed faintly blue before fading into nothing.

Tate didn't speak. He just stayed there, kneeling beside him, head bowed slightly as though in prayer.

"You're not a miracle worker, Ethan," he said quietly. "You're the bridge. Between what was taken... and what's returning."

Ethan stared at him, his breath trembling. The words didn't make him feel better, but they made a terrible kind of sense. He could feel it inside, the current that wanted out, that wanted connection. It wasn't just power; it was memory. The hum of the world trying to wake up through him.

He leaned forward, elbows on his knees, and whispered, "Then I'll hold as long as I can."

The candle flared. The blue light brightened until it washed through the chapel, catching the edges of the cross above the altar. For a second, the wood seemed to tremble, or maybe it was just the shimmer of reflected light.

Hogan pressed closer to Ethan's leg, whining once and going still.

The storm eased. The thunder moved farther away, leaving the sound of the creek outside whispering beneath the rain.

Tate rose slowly. His knees creaked; his face looked older now, or maybe just humbled by the sight.

"You'll hold," he said. "Until the others find you."

Ethan looked up, eyes still wet, light flickering in their depths. "Others?"

Tate nodded. "There are always others. The Weave doesn't thread itself through one man alone."

Ethan exhaled, long and tired. "Guess I'll believe that when I see it."

"You already have," Tate said, turning toward the door.

Ethan frowned, confused, but before he could speak, another roll of thunder rippled across the hills, and the last of the candlelight went out.

The stained glass continued to glow softly in the dark, colors like slow lightning, painting both men in shifting blue and gold.

They stood in silence, the air thick with something unspoken, grief, grace, or both.

And somewhere in the quiet beneath the rain, the Weave hummed again, steady, endless, alive.

The last of the thunder rolled off into the distance, swallowed by the hills.

The candle between them flickered once, its small flame fighting the draft that slipped through the broken panes, then steadied. The color shifted subtly, deepening from gold to white, then to a faint, impossible blue.

It wasn't bright enough to blind, just enough to make the shadows lean back, watching. The flame stood motionless, silent, perfect. Inside that tiny heart of fire, something moved, a pulse, a rhythm too deliberate to be chance.

Ethan watched it, barely breathing. Tate stood beside him, reverent and wordless. The hum that had haunted the air all night softened into something slower, gentler. Hogan let out a quiet sigh and laid his head down again, the tension gone from his body.

The light stayed. Not holy, not human. Just *alive*.

Outside, the storm was dying.

Inside, something older than faith began to breathe again.

22

The Cost of Miracles

The first thing Ethan noticed was the sound. Not the wind through the cracks in the walls or the slow drip of rain through the roof, but the deep, steady rhythm that pulsed inside him, like a second heartbeat that didn't belong to his body.

He sat at the edge of the cot, sweat slicking his back, breath hitching with every beat. His veins glowed faintly blue beneath the skin, the light waxing and fading in time with the invisible hum that filled the room. The pulse wasn't mechanical or human; it was alive.

Hogan paced the warped floorboards, nails clicking an uneven rhythm.

"I'm fine," Ethan muttered.

The words fell flat. He wasn't.

For two days he'd told himself otherwise. *Fine. Stable. Holding on.* But the truth was that his body was failing. Every act of healing, every miracle, had left its mark. The Weave, whatever force had chosen him, was consuming him cell by cell, breath by breath.

He leaned back against the wall. The old ranger cabin creaked under his weight, damp and cold. Tate's Bible still sat open on the chair beside the cot, its underlined verse staring back at him:

Five Hands shall rise when the world forgets its pulse.

He hadn't slept longer than an hour at a time. Whenever he drifted, he slipped into a place between dreaming and dying, a space of white threads, humming light, and the low whisper of voices calling from beyond the edge of sleep.

He flexed his hands. Light crawled beneath the surface of his skin, tracing the lines of his veins like rivers of fire. He pressed them flat against the table until the trembling stopped. When he lifted them, faint blue prints lingered, glowing for a heartbeat before fading.

"God help me," he whispered.

The boards beneath his feet vibrated in reply.

He moved through the day in fragments. Feeding Hogan. Pouring water into a rusted basin. Trying to find silence. But the silence itself hummed now, a low, living resonance that wouldn't let go.

The Weave was awake here. He could feel it in the air, that dense pressure before lightning strikes, that strange heaviness that makes the world hold its breath.

He splashed water on his face, leaned over the basin, and froze. His reflection shimmered. His eyes were different, irises faintly rimmed with pale light, as if they'd learned to catch what others couldn't see.

"You're not losing it," he told himself. "You're just... adapting."

But even as he said it, he knew. The heartbeat in his chest wasn't his anymore. It belonged to something older, larger, something that had claimed him.

By noon, the tremors worsened. Every time he touched metal, sparks jumped. Hogan barked at the doorway, hackles up, tail low.

Then came the hum.

The low vibration grew until it filled the cabin, shaking dust from the rafters. It was the same sound he'd felt under his skin for weeks, now magnified.

Ethan fell to his knees, clutching the cot frame. The air thickened, vibrating. The glow beneath his skin brightened until he could see bones through flesh.

Pain hit him in a wave, deep, cellular, as though his body were a field of live wires tearing apart from the inside.

The light flared, blinding, pure, and then the pain stopped.

He hit the floor hard, chest heaving, vision tunneling. Dust floated above him in slow suspension, each particle outlined in faint light.

The hum steadied, low and steady as breath. Not hostile, not kind. Simply *alive*.

He closed his eyes. The world went white.

When he opened them again, he wasn't in the cabin.

He floated in a vast lattice of light, a web of blue and silver stretching over an infinite darkness. The threads pulsed like veins, converging into glowing nodes that flared and dimmed with steady rhythm. Each pulse pulled at something deep inside his chest.

He reached out, and the Weave responded, threads shivering under his touch.

Then, through the endless light, came others.

A heartbeat like wildfire, fierce and restless.

A woman's voice carried through wind and dust.

Somewhere north, the air cracked with electricity, and the hum of machinery sang in harmony.

Another pulse, steady, strong, the rhythm of compassion itself.

They weren't faces, but *presences*, distinct, alive. He could feel their confusion, their pain, their awakening.

Four others.

And then the darkness.

A hollow void at the Weave's center, devouring the light around it. No pulse, no sound, only silence so deep it felt like gravity.

The other lights bent toward it, threads trembling. He felt the pull in his bones.

The Weave wasn't power, it was balance. And it was unraveling.

He reached for the light, but it receded, swallowed by shadow. When the darkness pulsed, the sound of his heartbeat disappeared. Then, white silence.

Kemen stood before him.

She looked dimmer now, as if even light could age. The brilliance that once burned through her had softened into a glow that flickered like a candle in wind.

"You've seen them," she said.

Ethan nodded weakly. "The others."

"They're waking," she said. "The Weave remembers its shape. But the burden remains with you until they are ready."

He forced a bitter laugh. "Ready? They didn't ask for this. None of us did."

Her gaze lowered. "I know."

"Then why me?" he said, voice breaking. "Why *any* of us?"

Kemen stepped closer, her light trembling. "Because the world needed hearts that knew loss. Only those who've broken can bear creation's pain."

He stared at her, unable to speak. Her words weren't comfort. They were truth, heavy and merciless.

"You're dying," she whispered.

He closed his eyes. "I can feel it."

"The Weave burns through you faster now," she said. "You carry more life than a single body can hold. The balance must be restored, or everything ends with you."

He looked up sharply. "You mean if I die,"

She shook her head. "If you die *without choosing*."

He laughed again, hollow, exhausted. "You sound like one of those preachers I used to tune out."

Her lips curved in something like a smile. "They were listening to echoes of me."

She reached out, touched his chest. The contact wasn't heat, but memory, warmth that filled him from the inside out.

For an instant, he saw her not as divine, but human. Weary. Grieving. Her light flickered once more before dimming.

"You can end this," she said, voice fading. "Or everything ends with you."

Then she was gone.

Only the imprint of her hand remained, a glowing sigil faintly burning over his heart, shaped like five lines branching from a single circle.

By dusk, the rain had returned.

Ethan stood in the doorway, duffel bag slung over his shoulder, the sky dark and trembling. Hogan sat beside him, tail thumping, slow and steady.

The glow beneath his skin had dimmed, but it was still there, a reminder with every breath.

"You don't have to come," he told Hogan.

The dog tilted his head, unbothered.

Ethan smiled, tired and small. "Didn't think so."

He climbed into Tate's truck. The seat groaned under his weight. The ignition coughed twice before catching. Headlights cut through the mist, scattering droplets into spectral arcs.

The world outside shimmered faintly. Trees bowed with invisible wind; the air itself seemed charged. On the horizon, streaks of blue-white light stitched the clouds like veins beneath skin.

He drove toward it.

Every mile hummed with the Weave's rhythm, his heartbeat syncing to the pulse beneath the earth. The road twisted through rain-slicked hills, leading him back toward the only place this could end.

If this is what it takes, he thought, gripping the wheel tighter, *then so be it.*

Hogan leaned against his leg. The hum inside him steadied.

The storm thickened overhead, and the sky ahead flashed with silent lightning, branching outward in five luminous lines that vanished as quickly as they came.

Ethan didn't look away.

The road home shone faintly beneath the storm's glow, as if the world itself was waiting for him to finish what it started.

Ethan's truck a small, lone glow winding through the darkness as veins of light pulse across the sky, converging slowly toward one point: Woodlawn.

23

Return to Woodlawn

The sun came up pale over the Tennessee hills, a thin ribbon of gold pushing through low fog. Ethan's truck rattled along the back road, the tires whispering over damp gravel. Every mile closer to home felt heavier. His hands trembled on the wheel, veins faintly luminous beneath the skin, the pulse of the Weave syncing with his heartbeat like a second rhythm only he could hear.

The familiar fence posts appeared, half-leaning, coated in moss. The air smelled of wet cedar and smoke from distant burn piles. Woodlawn had always been quiet, one of those small pockets of the world that seemed untouched by time, but now even that silence felt changed. It wasn't stillness anymore; it was listening.

When he crested the last rise, the cabin came into view. The roof had caved in near the chimney. Boards hung loose from the porch. A shutter banged weakly in the breeze. What had been a home now looked like something the storm had half-devoured and left to die.

Ethan parked near the oak stump and sat for a moment, engine ticking as it cooled. Hogan's head rose from the passenger seat, ears pricked, eyes bright. The dog whined once, soft, questioning.

"Yeah," Ethan whispered. "We made it back."

He opened the door. The air hit him like a current, charged, clean, almost electric. The creek that wound behind the house shimmered in the morning light, the surface glassy and alive with shifting color. Not reflection, something deeper, faint strands of blue and white weaving just beneath the water like living threads.

Hogan jumped down and padded toward it, tail wagging once before he froze, nose twitching at the hum. Ethan followed slowly. His boots sank in the mud near the bank, and when he crouched, he could feel it, the vibration in the ground, steady as a heartbeat. The Weave. Waiting.

He'd felt it for weeks, everywhere he went, a presence under everything, whispering through wires and storms, but here it was pure, raw, unfiltered. The place where it had first touched him.

The cabin groaned behind him as the wind picked up. He turned, took in the splintered porch steps, the collapsed roofline. He reached for the porch rail out of habit and stopped short when it pulsed beneath his palm, wood fibers glowing faintly, threads of light spreading out like veins from where he touched.

He drew back quickly. The light dimmed, leaving a faint heat behind.

Ethan exhaled slowly. "Guess it remembers me."

The sound of his own voice startled him; it felt small against the vast hum of the land. He walked through the open doorway, what was left of it, and into the shell of the cabin. Morning light poured through the broken roof, falling across dust and splintered beams. The bed was soaked from rain, the floor still streaked with mud. His small table was overturned, the Bible and notebook scattered across the boards, pages curled and stuck together.

He set them upright again, straightened the chair as though it mattered. Hogan nosed through the debris, sniffing every shadow, tail low.

"You smell it too, huh?" Ethan said quietly.

He could feel the energy pulsing through the walls, the floor, the air. The Weave wasn't just alive, it was *aware*. It watched him through the hum, curious and patient, as if waiting for a command.

He stepped back onto the porch, staring out at the hills. The fog was lifting, torn in ribbons by the light. Every tree branch dripped with moisture, reflecting glints of blue-white where sunlight met the invisible current.

He felt the fatigue deep in his bones now, the steady, throbbing ache that had been building since the highway crash. His body was burning itself out, cellular energy pushed beyond limits. Each breath shimmered faintly in the cool air, visible even without his exhale.

He sat on the porch step. Hogan came to rest beside him, pressing against his leg. Ethan reached down and ran his hand over the dog's head; warmth pulsed there too, steady and alive.

"Guess we're both running on borrowed time," he murmured.

The words didn't sound sad, not even resigned. They were simple truth.

A crow called somewhere beyond the creek, a single hoarse caw that echoed strangely. He looked up. More birds circled above the tree line, dozens, maybe hundreds, turning in a loose spiral. Their flight was slow, deliberate, almost ritualistic.

Ethan's pulse synced with their motion. The light beneath his skin flickered in time with each turn. He watched them until they dissolved into the horizon, leaving only the whisper of wings in the distance.

He leaned back against the porch post and closed his eyes. The hum grew clearer, separating into layers, tones within tones, like chords struck on a massive unseen instrument. Beneath them, faint words threaded through, impossible yet understood.

It is near. The line closes.

His eyes snapped open. The voice wasn't Kemen's; it was the Weave itself, resonant and impersonal. A warning, or a summons.

He rubbed his temples, the old instinct of a medic trying to shake off fatigue. "Not yet," he whispered. "Just let me rest a bit."

The hum subsided slightly, though not out of obedience. It felt more like compassion.

He stayed like that for a long while, letting the stillness wash through him. When he finally rose, his knees cracked. The creek shimmered again, light deepening to indigo as the sun climbed higher. He caught his reflection, flickering, blurred, like heat ripples.

The face that looked back at him wasn't the same man who'd left this place weeks ago. His eyes glowed faintly under the surface, the pupils rimmed in light. His skin carried that inner shimmer that no longer faded in daylight.

He looked both more alive and less human.

He took a slow breath, let it out. "All right," he said softly. "I'm home."

The words settled in the air like a benediction.

Behind him, the wind shifted direction, carrying a faint scent of honeysuckle and ozone. Hogan barked once, ears pricked. Somewhere far to the south, thunder rolled, a long, low growl that didn't sound entirely natural.

Ethan looked up. The sky above the hills shimmered faintly, as though light were bleeding through from somewhere beyond.

The Weave was moving again. And it was waiting for him.

The sound reached him first, the slow crunch of tires on gravel, cautious, hesitant. Ethan turned from the creek, hand still resting on the porch rail. Hogan's ears perked up. A moment later, the familiar shape of a silver Subaru eased around the bend in the road.

He felt his stomach tighten. For a second, he thought about retreating inside, about pretending he wasn't here, but there was nowhere to hide. The car rolled to a stop beside the split-rail fence. The engine shut off.

Lila stepped out.

She wore jeans spattered with mud and a rain jacket thrown on over her scrubs, her auburn hair tied back messily. Her boots sank into the wet ground as she shut the door. For a long moment, they just looked at each other across the yard, two ghosts trying to remember how to speak.

"You shouldn't be here," Ethan said finally. His voice was rough, quieter than he meant it to be.

Lila gave a small, hollow smile. "Neither should you."

She started toward him, stepping carefully over the debris, the broken boards that littered the path. Her eyes flicked to the cabin, taking in the damage, the half-collapsed roof. She looked back at him, and something in her gaze softened, relief mixed with fear.

"I saw the lights from the highway," she said. "Figured it was a flare, or maybe... maybe you."

Her voice trembled slightly at the end, but she steadied it. When she reached the steps, she hesitated, as though crossing an invisible threshold.

"Is it safe?" she asked.

Ethan almost smiled. "As safe as it gets."

That earned a faint laugh from her, tired, brittle, but real. She climbed the steps, pausing when she got close enough to touch him. Her eyes scanned his face, the faint luminescence beneath the skin of his throat, the pulse of blue-white light that came and went like the flicker of lightning behind clouds.

"You look," she started, then stopped, unable to finish.

"Yeah," he said. "I know."

She reached out before she could talk herself out of it, fingertips brushing the side of his face. His skin was fever-warm. The glow flared beneath her touch, brighter for an instant, casting faint reflections on her wrist.

She jerked her hand back instinctively, eyes wide, but didn't step away. "It's in you," she whispered.

Ethan nodded once. "It's always been. I just didn't know what to call it."

The wind shifted again, carrying the smell of rain and mud. A branch creaked somewhere in the woods. Hogan walked over and pressed his nose against Lila's hand, breaking the tension.

"Hey there, buddy," she murmured, scratching behind his ear. The normalcy of the motion, the simple, wordless affection, seemed to anchor them both for a moment.

When she straightened, Ethan motioned toward what was left of the porch swing. "You can sit, if it holds."

They sat side by side, the boards groaning under their weight. For a long while, neither spoke. The only sound was the creek murmuring in the distance, the soft crackle of shifting wood.

Finally, Lila said, "My house got hit in the storm. A tree came down right through the kitchen. Power's been out since last night."

He looked at her sharply. "You okay?"

She nodded. "Shaken up. Not hurt. The generator wouldn't start, so I went driving toward the ridge, then I saw this glow from here." She looked at him. "I thought it might be you. Or something worse."

Ethan glanced toward the creek, where the light pulsed faintly beneath the surface like veins beneath skin. "You weren't wrong."

She studied him, searching his face for the man she used to see, the quiet, awkward veteran who came into her clinic with stray dogs and mumbled thanks under his breath. That man was still there, but changed, blurred by something vast moving through him.

"I almost didn't stop," she said softly. "I didn't know what I'd find. But I couldn't just... not."

He swallowed hard. "You shouldn't have come."

"I couldn't stay away," she said.

The words hung between them, fragile as glass.

Ethan looked down, hands clasped between his knees. The faint light under his skin pulsed through the cracks in his knuckles, ghostly and rhythmic. "Everything's coming apart," he said. "I can feel it. Like a current that's too strong to stand in."

"Then let me help," she said.

He shook his head. "You can't. Nobody can."

She reached out again, this time laying her hand on his wrist. The warmth there was startling, almost painful. But she didn't move. "You think I haven't seen people burn themselves out trying to save others? That's half my job. You don't have to do this alone."

His eyes lifted to hers. "I already am."

Hogan whined softly, sensing the shift in tone. Lila turned to him, scratching the dog's head absently. "He's still loyal," she said. "Still follows you everywhere."

"Yeah," Ethan murmured. "He's smarter than I am."

Lila's laugh was short, choked by tears she didn't want to shed. "You're impossible."

"I'm dying," Ethan said quietly. "That's different."

The bluntness of it froze her. The air between them seemed to thin. She looked at him, really looked, and saw it now: the exhaustion hollowing his face, the faint tremor in his hands, the pulse under his skin like lightning trying to escape.

"No," she whispered. "There has to be a way,"

Ethan cut her off gently. "Not this time."

The words were final, but not cruel. They were simply the truth, and it hung there between them with terrible clarity.

The silence stretched. Hogan laid his head on Ethan's boot, tail thumping once. Somewhere above them, a hawk cried out, circling the ridge.

Ethan looked out toward the hills. "You ever feel like you can hear the world breathing?"

Lila followed his gaze. "What do you mean?"

He gestured toward the trees, the shifting light, the creek. "All of this, it's alive, connected. I can feel it now, every heartbeat, every gust of wind. It's like... it's waiting for me to finish something I started without knowing I did."

Her throat tightened. "That sounds like faith."

He smiled faintly. "Feels more like gravity."

They sat in silence again, watching the light move along the creek's surface, twisting in patterns that no current could explain.

The wind carried the faintest hum, not loud, but enough to raise the hairs on their arms. Lila shivered, though not from cold.

"Ethan," she said quietly. "What's happening to you?"

He looked down at his hands. The glow pulsed once more, faint but insistent. "It's not just me anymore," he said. "It's the world. It's... waking up."

Lila didn't understand, not fully, but she nodded anyway, because in his voice she heard something both terrifying and true.

They stayed there until the light began to shift toward noon, the air thick with everything left unsaid. When she finally spoke again, her voice was soft, almost reverent.

"I was afraid you'd be gone," she said.

He looked at her. "I still might be."

The faintest smile touched her lips, sad and real. "Then I'll stay until you are."

Ethan didn't answer. He just watched the water glinting in the sunlight, and for the first time since this all began, he felt something like peace, fragile, fleeting, but real enough to hold onto a little while longer.

Afternoon light slipped through the gaps in the roof like pale ribbons, dust and pollen swirling in its path. The sound of the creek outside carried through the open window, slow, rhythmic, unhurried, the same cadence Ethan's heart was trying to mimic.

He sat at the small kitchen table, now cracked down one leg, the grain of the wood veined with faint blue light. Lila had cleared a space, pushing aside the broken lamp and a few scattered papers. She poured what was left of the coffee from her thermos into two chipped mugs.

"Still warm," she said quietly.

Ethan nodded. "Appreciate it."

He wrapped his hands around the cup but didn't drink. The heat from his skin was stronger than the coffee's; it made the porcelain tremble. A small ring of condensation formed where his fingers touched, shimmering faintly before evaporating.

Lila watched, saying nothing. Hogan lay at their feet, eyes half-closed, tail flicking lazily every so often. The air felt charged, a hum rising just below hearing.

Finally, Lila broke the silence. "You said this place feels alive."

He looked up. "It is. Everything is."

"The light?" she asked. "The storms?"

He nodded slowly. "All connected. The Weave, it's what holds everything together. Energy, thought, life, it's all the same current, just different frequencies." He paused, glancing at his hands. "But something's wrong. The balance broke when magic, or whatever you want to call it, came back. I can feel the tear growing."

"The tear?"

"Like a wound in the world," he said. "Every storm, every surge, every death I feel, it's all the same pressure trying to escape."

She leaned forward, voice trembling. "And you think you can fix it?"

He met her eyes. "No. I *know* I can."

Lila shook her head. "That's not the same thing."

Ethan's faint smile didn't reach his eyes. "I've been feeling it since the facility, the way it threads through me. It's not just in me, Lila. I've become a conduit. My body's feeding the current, grounding it. It's why I'm still alive. For now."

Her breath caught. "For now?"

He exhaled, steady but soft. "The energy's eating through me. My heart's overclocked. Cells regenerating faster than they should. I'm burning out, cell by cell."

Lila stood, pacing to the broken window. The light outside flickered, like clouds crossing the sun, but when she looked up, there were no clouds at all. Just light shifting, bending, like air over heat.

She turned back to him, voice cracking. "You can't just die for it. There has to be another way."

Ethan's gaze was steady. "There isn't. Not for me."

Her hands balled into fists. "You're talking about suicide."

He shook his head. "Sacrifice. There's a difference."

"Don't you dare make it sound noble."

He didn't respond. He just stared at the light spilling across the table, watching how it pulsed faintly with each beat of his heart.

Lila came closer, voice breaking. "You've saved lives, Ethan. You brought that boy back. You brought Hogan back. If you can do all that, why not save yourself?"

He looked up slowly. "Because the current needs somewhere to go. And if I don't release it, it'll tear through everything. The Weave's unstable, like a dam about to burst. If it fails completely..."

He trailed off.

"What happens?"

"The world burns from the inside out," he said quietly. "No fire. Just collapse. The pulse stops."

Lila stared at him, trying to process words that didn't fit any world she understood. "So what, you just... walk into the light and hope it fixes itself?"

His lips twitched, a ghost of a smile. "Something like that."

She stepped closer, shaking her head. "You're not some chosen one, Ethan. You're a man. You bleed, you ache, you *matter*."

He met her gaze with quiet gentleness. "And that's exactly why it has to be me."

Her breath shuddered out. She leaned against the counter, eyes glassy with unshed tears. Hogan lifted his head, sensing her distress, tail thumping once.

Ethan reached out and rested a trembling hand on the dog's back. "It's okay, boy."

Lila turned to face him again. "You said you were no savior."

"I'm not," Ethan said. "I'm just a medic patching up what broke."

The simplicity of it hit her harder than any sermon could have. She pressed her hand to her mouth, trying to hold back the sob rising in her throat.

"You can't do this," she whispered. "You can't ask me to watch you die."

He rose slowly from the chair, every movement measured, deliberate. The veins in his arms shimmered faintly beneath the skin, blue-white lines tracing like rivers of light. When he stepped closer, she felt the air vibrate.

He raised a hand, hesitated, then brushed her cheek with his fingertips. His touch was hot, not fever, but the kind of warmth that felt alive, elemental. The glow spread across her skin where he touched, then faded again.

"You helped me remember I was human," he said softly.

Her eyes closed, tears escaping despite her effort. "That's not enough reason to let go."

"It's the only reason that matters," he said.

The wind rose suddenly, rattling the walls. The creek outside began to hum louder, not rushing faster, but resonating, as though the very water recognized what was coming. Dust lifted from the floorboards, swirling around their feet in tiny spirals of light.

Lila looked around, startled. "Ethan..."

He glanced upward. "It's starting."

"What is?"

"The Weave. It's responding."

Outside, the trees began to sway though no wind reached the ground. The air thickened, the low hum becoming a tone that seemed to vibrate in their chests.

Lila's voice shook. "You said there were others, people like you."

He nodded. "I can feel them now. Waking up. Scattered. But I was the first. The anchor."

"And what happens when you let go?"

He hesitated, eyes distant. "Then it's up to them."

The look on his face was not fear but clarity, the steady resolve of someone who had already made peace with what came next.

The light through the roof beams grew brighter, turning the dust into motes of color that drifted between them like slow-moving stars. Lila could feel the charge in the air, the same energy she'd felt the night at the clinic when Hogan defied death, multiplied a hundred-fold.

She took a step back, voice trembling. "You'll die."

He gave a small nod. "Probably."

She choked on a laugh that wasn't really a laugh. "You make it sound easy."

"It's not," he said quietly. "But it's right."

The hum outside deepened, the creek glowing faintly through the doorway. Hogan stood, tail rigid, watching the water. The world seemed to lean forward, listening.

Lila wiped her eyes with the back of her sleeve. "Then what do I do?"

Ethan looked at her, really looked, and smiled faintly. "Remember. Tell them I wasn't a miracle. Just a medic."

Her breath hitched. "You think anyone's going to believe that?"

He shrugged, weary amusement in his eyes. "Doesn't matter. You will."

The sound outside built into a low roar, the kind that came before lightning split the sky. Lila could feel it now, the pulse running through the floor, up the walls, through her own heartbeat.

"Ethan,"

He raised a hand gently, silencing her. "It's okay. It's already begun."

A gust of wind tore through the cabin, scattering dust and papers into a spiraling column. Light from the creek spilled through the doorway, crawling up the walls like liquid fire.

Lila stepped closer, but he shook his head. His eyes, when he looked at her, were almost entirely light.

"Go outside," he said softly. "You shouldn't see this from in here."

Her throat worked soundlessly, but she obeyed. As she stepped onto the porch, the hum reached its crescendo. The air shimmered. The forest seemed to hold its breath.

Behind her, Ethan stood in the doorway, haloed by light.

She turned, tears streaking her face, and whispered, "Don't do this."

He smiled gently, the kind of smile that broke her heart because it was so calm. "It's already done."

The glow surged through the cabin like a heartbeat, spilling into the trees. Lila felt it in her bones, a pressure, vast and alive, gathering for release.

And in that blinding quiet before it burst, she thought she heard him whisper, not to her, but to the world itself:

"Let it mend."

The sound grew to a deafening hum, then beyond hearing altogether, a vibration felt more in the chest than the ears. The entire creek was molten brilliance now, spilling light up into the trees, into the clouds, into the sky itself.

For a heartbeat, Ethan stood in the center of it, arms spread slightly, head tilted back, not in pain, but release. His outline flickered, solid one moment, pure radiance the next.

Lila tried to reach him, but the air between them shimmered with heat and force. Her voice tore from her throat. "Ethan!"

He didn't answer.

The light expanded, a silent detonation that rolled outward across the forest. Trees bent like grass in a gale. The hum reached a crescendo, and then, all at once, collapsed into silence.

Everything went still.

The light withdrew like breath, folding back into the creek. The water ran clear again, as if nothing had happened. The trees stood motionless. Even the air seemed hesitant to move.

Lila stood frozen, hand half-raised, mouth open but no sound coming out. The glow faded from her skin, leaving only the ghost of warmth.

"Ethan..." she whispered.

But there was no answer.

She stumbled forward to the creek's edge. The water reflected her face in broken ripples, tear-streaked, pale, hollow-eyed. Hogan followed, pressing against her side, whining softly. She sank to her knees, fingers digging into the wet mud.

The current lapped gently at the bank, perfectly calm, perfectly ordinary.

Only when she looked closer did she see it, faint lines etched into the surface of the water itself, glowing just below sight: five intersecting paths forming a circle. They pulsed once, softly, then dimmed.

The Weave was sealed.

Lila bowed her head, shoulders shaking. Hogan whined again, resting his head in her lap.

The wind picked up, carrying the smell of rain and cedar. In the distance, the hills shimmered faintly, reflecting the last traces of blue-white light, visible for miles, maybe hundreds. Somewhere, she imagined, people were stepping out of their homes, staring at the sky and wondering what they were seeing.

But here, by the creek, all was still.

She reached out and touched the water. It was warm. A faint hum vibrated against her fingertips, gentle, steady, like a heartbeat.

"Rest easy, medic," she whispered.

The words carried across the water, and for an instant, the reflection beside her shifted, a flicker of light in the shape of a man, hand raised in farewell. Then it was gone.

Above, the sky deepened to indigo. The first stars appeared, their light barely visible against the faint blue glow that lingered over the valley, the last breath of the Weave settling back into the world.

The wind sighed through the trees, soft and low, like an exhale.

And somewhere in that sound, just beyond hearing, came a whisper that might have been a voice, calm, familiar, eternal.

"*We're still here.*"

24

Resolution and Legacy

The silence after death was not empty.

It was vast, breathing, alive.

Light spread in every direction, white that wasn't color but consciousness itself, a current of memory and motion stretching forever. The sensation of gravity, of body, of heartbeat had all vanished, and yet something of Ethan still *was*. He floated, no, he *drifted*, in an ocean made of pulse and sound, threads of radiance weaving and unweaving around him like living veins.

Somewhere in that blinding expanse, a voice murmured. Not in English, not in any human language, but he knew it meant *You did it.*

The threads shivered. The light pulled into form.

And Kemen appeared.

She rose from the brightness like a figure emerging from surf, tall and radiant, her hair flowing as if caught in celestial wind. Her expression was sorrow and serenity bound together. The Weave glowed through her skin, faint runes drifting across her arms like constellations come alive.

"*Well done, Heart of Life,*" she said. Her voice wasn't sound; it was the echo of his own pulse answering back.

Ethan tried to speak, but no air came. He looked down, saw not hands but shapes of light, outlines flickering like candle flames in a breeze. His body was gone. What remained was an imprint, a resonance of who he had been.

"Is this... heaven?" he asked, though it came out more as thought than speech.

Kemen smiled, the kind that made the light around her soften. "There are no heavens, only homes. You returned yours to balance."

He looked down through the ocean of light, and below, so far below it made him dizzy, he saw the curve of the Earth. Clouds shimmered silver where storms still roamed. From horizon to horizon ran faint filaments of blue-white, connecting rivers, forests, cities. The Weave.

"You were never meant to carry it alone," Kemen said, stepping closer. "No heart can hold creation without breaking."

"Then why give it to me?" His voice trembled, not from fear, but from exhaustion that felt older than life.

"You were not given it," she said. "You answered it. Life called for a medic, and you came."

He almost laughed, if laughter could exist here. "It hurt like hell."

Kemen reached out, her hand glowing brighter as she touched his shoulder. The light from her palm flowed through him, threads of memory unraveling: the creek, Lila's face, Hogan's bark, the sound of his own heart in the dark. They didn't vanish; they simply joined the light.

"Pain is the proof of purpose," Kemen said softly. "Even we forgot that once."

He met her gaze. "Is it over?"

"For now."

She looked upward, and the light shifted. Above them, if direction even meant anything here, a vast, circular shape appeared: five intersecting lines radiating from a central point, runes pulsing at their tips. One of them, the line glowing brightest, matched the hue of Ethan's light.

"The seal holds again," Kemen said. "But it has changed. What you gave back cannot be unmade."

He understood, though no words were needed. Magic, life, the pulse of the world, it was all moving again. Humanity would feel it, not as miracles, but as potential.

"Will they be ready?" he asked.

Kemen's eyes darkened with something like worry. "Readiness is an illusion. They will *learn,* as they always have, through wonder, and through ruin."

The Weave pulsed once, a slow heartbeat through the light. Ethan felt himself thinning, dispersing, each pulse carrying away another piece of what he had been.

Kemen's expression broke then, divine composure cracking into grief. "You cannot stay here," she whispered. "Your energy belongs to the cycle."

Ethan looked down again, to the world below, the blue glow tracing rivers, the mountains shining faintly as dawn moved across continents. Somewhere down there, in a valley by a Tennessee creek, a woman would wake and listen for a hum that would never quite fade.

He nodded. "Tell her... tell her I'm okay."

Kemen's reply was soft and heavy as the end of prayer. "She already knows."

The threads began to pull him apart, not painfully, but gently, like a tide reclaiming the sand. He closed his eyes and let it take him.

Light poured through him. He wasn't Ethan anymore, but he wasn't gone. He was warmth, pulse, current. He was in the water, the soil, the breath of the wind that carried voices too faint for human ears.

"Rest," Kemen said. Her tears scattered into light. "You've mended what we broke."

The Weave shimmered in response, brighter and wider, rippling outward until even Kemen had to shield her eyes. And when she looked again, he was gone, his form scattered into the endless lattice of living light.

The last trace of his voice brushed her thoughts like a whisper carried on the edge of a storm.

"It's all right now."

Kemen stood alone in the glow for a long time, watching the new currents thread across the world below. For the first time in millennia, she allowed herself to hope, and to fear.

Because balance restored was never permanent.
And life, once awakened, would never sleep again.

The light folded inward, and Kemen stood once more in the chamber of the Well.

Stone arched above her, vast and ancient, its carvings older than the memory of mankind. The well itself glowed with quiet majesty, a miniature Earth turning slowly in a pool of light, the blue lines of the Weave pulsing across its surface like veins beneath translucent skin.

Around her, the others gathered.

Vilya appeared first, robed in shadowed silver, his eyes pale as winter skies. Beagron followed, shoulders like carved granite, his beard streaked with gold and gray. Cylian drifted into being as a column of green light before coalescing into a figure cloaked in living moss. Last came Antec, tall, austere, a crown of flame shimmering faintly above his brow.

They stood in silence, watching the Earth spin below them. The hum of the Weave was everywhere now, a low music reverberating through the stones, neither ominous nor peaceful, something older than either.

"It is done," Vilya said at last, his voice carrying the stillness of deep caverns. "The seal has re-formed."

"Yes," Kemen replied quietly. "But it is not what it was."

Beagron's hand tightened on the edge of the stone rim. "You mean the mortal changed it."

Kemen nodded. "He gave back what we took. Not as we did, out of fear, but out of mercy. His act left the Weave open, not sealed. Contained, but alive."

Cylian's gaze flickered toward the glowing sphere. "The light runs through all things again. The forests whisper it. The roots remember."

"And the oceans stir," Antec added, his voice rumbling like distant thunder. "Even the volcanoes sing. The world breathes anew."

"That breathing," Vilya said sharply, "may yet become fire. You all remember why we closed the Weave. What man did with power once, they will do again."

Kemen turned to him, her expression steady but mournful. "They will *choose* again, Vilya. That is what we denied them. Choice. We cannot guide life and call it free."

He glared back. "You speak of freedom. I speak of survival."

Beagron stepped between them. "Enough. Both of you. We have lost too much to argue over ashes."

Cylian's voice, soft and melodic, wove through the tension. "He is not ashes. He is part of the song now. Can you not hear it?"

They fell silent.

And for a moment, all five listened.

The hum beneath the world deepened, steady, rhythmic, pulsing. Through the image of Earth below, faint ripples of light spread, tracing the outlines of mountains, rivers, cities, and deserts. It was no longer the sterile weave they had bound; it was wild, unpredictable, alive.

"His heartbeat lingers," Kemen said. "The Heart of Life sustains the new pattern."

"Unsanctioned," Vilya muttered. "Unstable."

"Unstoppable," Beagron countered.

A faint smile touched Kemen's lips. "The difference between chaos and creation is whether one learns to listen."

The chamber brightened, as though the well itself responded to her words. The miniature Earth shimmered, its clouds forming strange spirals of light. Tiny points flared across continents, small, bright pulses where the Weave had touched mortal lives.

Vilya frowned. "These lights, what are they?"

"Echoes," Cylian whispered. "The energy he released has taken root. Healers who cure incurable wounds. Seeds that grow in poisoned soil. Machines that run without fuel. It has already begun."

Antec's flame dimmed to an ember. "Then our age of silence is ended."

"No," Kemen said softly, her gaze distant. "Only broken."

Vilya folded his arms, cloak swirling like storm clouds. "And when they come seeking gods again? When they build their weapons and their temples and call upon us to fix what they ruin?"

Beagron placed a heavy hand on his shoulder. "Then perhaps this time, they will find no gods at all, only their own reflection."

The words hung there, echoing.

The five immortals turned toward the well. Below, dawn passed from one horizon to the next, and the world rolled on. A thousand new beginnings sparked in the quiet places, unseen, uncelebrated.

Kemen rested her hand over the turning sphere. "The current is weaker now, but steady. The Weave has found its rhythm again."

Cylian nodded. "What was contained has become memory. What remains will become myth."

"And the Heart?" Beagron asked.

Kemen's eyes softened. "He rests where he began. In the current. In the hum of the world. His name will fade, but his echo will never leave."

The others bowed their heads, even Vilya, though reluctantly. The light from the well shimmered upward, casting the chamber in soft blue radiance.

For the first time in millennia, there was peace between them, not the peace of agreement, but of weary acceptance.

Kemen stepped back from the well. "Then we will watch again."

Beagron grunted. "And if the darkness stirs?"

Her gaze drifted upward toward the unseen heavens. "Then perhaps humanity will answer, not us."

The Weave pulsed once more, a slow, steady heartbeat spreading outward through the chamber, then across the cosmos itself.

Outside, through the invisible corridors of time and space, the light rippled across the stars. And far below, on the spinning world they had once sealed, dawn broke in a thousand places at once.

The age of silence was over.

And the world, still wounded, still imperfect, had begun to hum again.

****

The world woke to light.

It began just before dawn, filaments of blue-white radiance weaving through cloud banks from Beijing to Boston. The sky shimmered like water disturbed by breath, auroras dancing where they did not belong. Planes rerouted midflight. Satellites went blind for thirty seconds that no one could explain.

And then came the reports.

Hospitals in São Paulo and Seoul reported cardiac monitors flatlining, only to spike again, patients returning from brain death with no visible trauma. In a drought-stricken village in Kenya, dry wells overflowed with clear water. In Nevada, an abandoned silver mine lit from within like molten glass, veins of luminescent quartz spider-webbing through the rock.

Everywhere, the same phenomenon: things long broken mending themselves.

By midmorning, every screen on Earth carried the same headline, reshaped a hundred different ways:

"The Light Event."

"Miracle Dawn."

"The Moore Phenomenon."

News anchors spoke in carefully measured tones, balancing awe with skepticism. Clips replayed Ethan's rescue of the drowning boy, slowed and enhanced. Talk show panels filled with physicists, theologians, and military analysts, all claiming answers, none convincing.

"... atmospheric plasma resonance," one expert said, her face pale in studio lights.

"... spontaneous mass hysteria," another countered, though his voice trembled.

A grainy cell-phone video from rural Tennessee played again and again, trees bowing under a dome of radiant wind, the silhouette of a man by a creek vanishing into white light.

For every headline proclaiming *miracle,* another screamed *containment failure.*

For every prayer whispered in gratitude, there was another muttered in fear.

But amid the noise, there were quieter stories. A paralyzed child taking her first steps in a Houston hospital. Coral reefs blooming again in the Pacific. A power grid in Europe running three days without fuel.

Life, impossibly, was healing itself.

In a gray office in Washington, D.C., Agent Cole Ramirez stared at the footage looping silently across his monitor. He'd watched it a hundred times, each pass leaving him more hollow.

The containment facility lay in ruins now, a crater rimmed with glass. Yet not one of his team had died. Every agent pulled from the wreckage carried the same report: *there was light, then silence, then nothing hurt anymore.*

He leaned back, rubbing at the bridge of his nose.

The report he'd been asked to write sat unfinished on the screen:

SUBJECT: MOORE, ETHAN. STATUS: UNCONFIRMED DECEASED.

RESULT: PHENOMENON CLASSIFIED, BIOENERGETIC ANOMALY.

He couldn't make himself type the rest.

The hum still followed him. It wasn't in the walls or machines, it was *inside* him. A faint vibration under the ribs, matching his heartbeat. Sometimes, when the city was quiet, the light in his apartment flickered in rhythm with it.

He thought about the man in the video, the medic who had looked more afraid of his own gift than any weapon aimed at him.

Ramirez shut the laptop and rose. Outside his window, the city glowed under an unfamiliar sky, clouds edged in that same impossible blue.

He walked down the hall, past security checkpoints and empty offices, until he reached the Director's door. He didn't knock.

"I'm done," he said simply, badge already on the desk. "You can call it whatever you want, terrorism, divine event, energy anomaly. But I've seen what we are when we try to cage a miracle."

The Director didn't argue. He just stared at him with the weary look of a man who knew history was moving beyond his pay grade.

Ramirez stepped out into the street. The air felt charged, the kind of air before a storm, but this wasn't a storm. Streetlamps flickered as he passed, humming faintly in unison with his pulse.

He tilted his head back. The dawn sky shimmered faintly, a single long aurora stretching across the horizon like a living scar.

He whispered, "Rest easy, soldier."

And for a moment, he thought he heard an answer in the hum, a low, steady rhythm, neither word nor sound, but something deeper. Like a heartbeat.

He smiled, faintly, and walked on.

Across the world, the hum settled into the rhythm of ordinary life. The miraculous became part of weather reports, study abstracts, whispered prayers.

Children drew the five-lined rune in notebooks without knowing why. Electricity flowed cleaner. Crops grew taller. A new quiet spread, not peace exactly, but balance.

And far away, beyond the reach of satellites and sirens, Tennessee rolled into evening light.

The road to Woodlawn was quieter than she remembered.

Lila drove with the windows down, the wind moving through her hair in slow, whispering breaths. The air carried a faint charge, as if the world had only just finished exhaling after a long-held breath. She hadn't come here since the night the sky split open. For weeks, she'd avoided even the thought of it, afraid that returning might feel like re-opening a wound.

But the letters had started to arrive, strangers she'd never met, people claiming to have been healed, to have felt something "through the light." Some wrote to thank *him*. Some to demand answers. Others just wanted to know if he was real.

She never replied. What could she say?

Now, as her tires crunched over gravel and the trees parted, the cabin came into view, or what was left of it.

The structure had collapsed months ago. The roof had caved in under storm debris, the chimney toppled, windows shattered. But nature had already begun its quiet reclamation. Wildflowers covered the foundation in thick patches of white and violet. Grass grew in rippling green waves. The air smelled of rain and new earth.

And at the heart of it all, the creek flowed on.

It gleamed in the evening light, clear and slow, a soft blue shimmer visible beneath the surface. The same color she'd seen when Ethan vanished, the same hue that haunted her dreams.

She parked the car and stepped out, Hogan leaping down after her, tail wagging. The old dog was graying now, his movements slower but still steady. He walked ahead, nose to the ground, then stopped at the water's edge.

Lila followed.

The grass brushed against her jeans, wet with dew. The air hummed faintly, not a sound, but a pressure just beneath hearing, like the low vibration of a cello string. It seemed to pulse with her heartbeat.

She crouched near the creek, dipping her fingers into the current. It was cool and impossibly clean. The touch sent a shiver up her arm, a faint static warmth, almost familiar.

"Hey," she whispered. Her voice came out smaller than she meant it to. "It's been a while."

The creek murmured, the sound blending with wind in the trees. Somewhere a bird called, the tone pure and even.

"I don't know if you can hear me," she said, "but you did it. The world's... different now. Things are growing again. People are scared, but they're *living*."

Hogan settled beside her, chin on his paws, eyes fixed on the water. His reflection glowed faintly, like he, too, was part of the hum.

Lila smiled, faint and trembling. "You fixed it."

She closed her eyes. For a moment, there was nothing but the sound of water and the wind threading through branches. Then, somewhere in that quiet, soft, distant, she felt it. A pulse.

It wasn't sound. It was deeper.
Like something vast and unseen had just remembered her name.

Her breath caught. She looked up, heart hammering. The light around the meadow had changed, dusk spilling gold into blue, the edges blurring until it felt like the whole world had softened. The trees shimmered faintly, their leaves whispering to one another in a language just out of reach.

The creek glowed brighter for an instant. Five lines of light rippled across its surface, intersecting into a perfect circle before fading back into the current.

Lila's hand went to her chest. She smiled through her tears.

"Rest easy, medic."

A breeze swept through the meadow, carrying her words away. Hogan lifted his head, ears twitching, and for the briefest moment, just before the wind passed, the hum answered.

It was gentle, rhythmic, unmistakable.

A heartbeat.

Lila wiped her face, stood, and turned toward the car. The last of the sun slipped behind the hills, and the air filled with the scent of rain and honeysuckle.

Behind her, the creek flowed on, calm and luminous.
From high above, if one could see it from the stars, it traced a faint glowing circle, the same pattern that once bound the world.

And deep beneath the soil and water, the Weave pulsed softly, alive again.

The gods were silent once more.
But the earth had begun to sing.

I discovered storytelling as a child navigating foster care, where books became both refuge and inspiration. After serving twenty-four years in the U.S. Army with three combat deployments, I returned to writing, drawing on a lifetime of resilience, discipline, and imagination. I now live in rural Tennessee, where I write full-time. *Fractures in the Weave* is my debut novel.

www.ingramcontent.com/pod-product-compliance
Lightning Source LLC
Chambersburg PA
CBHW020039310726
48970CB00007B/2329